FOLLOW YOUR DREAMS

KAT RYAN

To my students, my sons, and my ten-year-old self who desperately wanted to be an author.

You can do anything you dream up.

ial{no}

TRAVELING UP THE ROAD

Elle

The road stretched in front of me over the ridge on this two-lane state highway and dipped to offer my first view of Highland Falls, a small town nestled straight ahead. I'd traded my Chicago skyline for trees, grain elevators, and a water tower. I couldn't wait.

My sister Ava had moved to the tiny town in central Illinois two years ago to follow her dream of teaching AP English at their local high school. We'd grown up in Indianapolis, about two and a half hours to the east. Ava swore that I'd find a community in a town of ten thousand people and feel far more at home here. I hoped to hell she was right.

I'd spent my twenties living in Chicago, thinking I'd go there and find success as a young author living in the city. That was *my* dream, after all.

What I found was rejection letter after rejection letter. I wanted to write historical fiction. Instead, I found myself working for an education publisher, doing marketing copy and some editing work. It paid the bills and was, frankly, sucking my soul dry.

Ava had called a month ago. I think she could tell I was struggling. In a city of almost three million people, I felt so damn alone. As I could do my job from anywhere, Ava begged me to move south.

You know that Willie Nelson song, "City of New Orleans"? she'd asked.

What on earth are you talking about?

Look it up, I'll wait.

Okay, got it. What's the point?

There's a train leaving Union Station called the City of New Orleans. That's what Willie is singing about. Get your ass on it and motor on down here. I'll meet you at the Champaign station.

So while I didn't hop on the train—I had a car, for God's sake—I did pack up and gave notice at my apartment complex. I'd been month to month on my lease for the past year, which might have been a sign had I been paying any attention.

Whatever.

Unlike Willie, I wouldn't be going five hundred miles before the day was done, just a little over a hundred. And while Ava said I could stay with her at her place, I'd found an apartment for rent over a little indie bookstore in the downtown of Ava's new home.

I loved my sister and all, but I was too old to crash on a couch. Besides, a bookstore as my downstairs neighbor? Yes please. I might be flat broke before the week was out, but I'd be happy.

Your destination is on the right in a quarter of a mile.

"Thanks, Linda."

Linda kept me on track, headed to my new home. At

some point on this drive, I'd named the voice from my GPS, wanting to have a conversation with someone. Troubling sign? I didn't think so.

Maybe I needed to consider a cat in my apartment. Or should I become one of those people who talks to houseplants? That seemed like a solid move; they wouldn't be as much work as a cat.

Or would they? Clearly I'd never owned either.

Taking a right, I drove straight onto a Hallmark movie set. I mean, what else could you call this quaint little town?

I slowed down, which was no issue since there didn't seem to be any traffic. Come to think of it, I hadn't passed a traffic light or stop sign on my way into town.

The drive in had wound through a residential neighborhood, but now I seemed to be in what this town might refer to as the business district. Old-fashioned acorn streetlamps just coming on lined the street in front of two-story, brick-faced buildings with businesses on the lower level, windows above. Ava had said that the second story of almost all the buildings downtown were small apartments and lofts.

After two blocks of businesses, the street opened up to a large building that took up the entire block to the left. A glance at the sign out front shared that this was the courthouse. White lights were strung around the town square, creating a warm glow. It wasn't quite dinnertime, so the sun hadn't completely set, but between the lights and streetlamps, the area was well lit.

"You've arrived at your destination."

"Thanks, Linda."

I looked to the right, and sure enough, there it was. The bookstore was also ridiculously adorable. The name was spelled out in large typewriter keys in the front window,

Pages. The green building and yellow front door were exactly what Ivy, the owner, had told me to look for.

I'd arrived indeed.

I glanced at my packed back seat. "Linda, thoughts? Pack mule on up and head in, or come out and do several trips?"

My cell's GPS remained silent because of course it did.

I nodded, soldiering on. "Yep. Solid call. Head on in, get the lay of the land along with a key from Ivy, then back out here. Thanks, Linda."

I really needed to ask Ivy about a cat. I mean, working from home was not going to help matters here.

I grabbed my phone and thumbed out a text to Ava announcing my arrival, then hopped out of my vehicle with a pat to the roof in thanks as I passed by. My old Subaru might not be sexy, but the station wagon had gotten me here safely.

I opened the door to step into Pages and heard the bell ring overhead.

"I'll be right with you," a voice called from the back.

I glanced around, trying to get the vibe for the store in one look. Part of my job was writing up descriptions for books, articles, and professional development sessions. I found myself practicing the skill often, everywhere I went.

Ivy's bookstore was perfection. Relaxed, chill, and comfortable were all descriptors that came to mind. There was a scent I couldn't place pervading the place. Sandalwood maybe? Wood floors gleamed with light bouncing off them. There was a counter where you paid to one side of the store with a chalkboard behind it. Glancing at it, I saw some reviews and recommendations for books posted as well as the diffuser that I figured was responsible for the welcoming scent. There was another counter against a wall in the back with what appeared to be a coffee maker and teapot. A hall led toward the back, where I'm guessing the voice that greeted me had called from.

Taking a deep breath, I felt myself relax from my drive down, from life in general. This place gave me the same feelings I had in our neighborhood library growing up. Ms. Rogers had worked there and welcomed me every Saturday morning, making me feel like she'd been waiting just for me.

Voices brought me back to the store, and I glanced up to see a younger version of Stevie Nicks enter the room, talking over her shoulder.

"Just bring that box up here after you stack the rest and we're good to go," she called back. Glancing my way, she smiled. "Elle?"

"How'd you know?"

Stevie moved toward me. "Ava showed me a picture of the two of you. Are you a hugger?"

She wrapped her arms around me and squeezed as I wondered if I'd nodded or not. I was, so it worked. She smelled like lavender, and I relaxed into her embrace. After working out of my apartment for so long, the interaction was welcome.

Letting go, I felt like I was missing something.

"I'm Ivy," Stevie said.

I laughed. "I was calling you Stevie in my head, but of course you're Ivy."

Her eyes lit up. "Stevie as in Stevie Nicks?"

I nodded.

Her laugh was glorious; it filled the space up. "I do love Fleetwood Mac." She moved behind the counter. "Let me get you the keys. Today's been crazy, sorry. My four-year-old, Addie, came down with a cold. My friend Emma is watching her so I could close up tonight and get you what you needed."

Looking over at Ivy, I was surprised to hear that she had a daughter, much less one that was already four. If she'd said she was following a band on tour this summer, yes, that would track. With Ivy's carefree spirit and long blond hair along with her hippie vibe, it was like she'd just walked out of some boho Instagram account. I wondered if her daughter was as laid-back as her.

"I'm sorry your daughter is sick. I hate that I put you out."

Ivy's laughter was contagious, and it warmed me up. "Goddess knows that I needed a break. Being with a four-year-old for any amount of focused time is exhausting. I love Ads to pieces, but the amount of questions she comes up with is unreal. We've had dance parties all day long, so this is a blessed break. Now"—she pulled open a drawer—"where are those keys?"

A deep voice came from behind me. "Ivy, the boxes are taken care of."

I looked to the new voice, and I'm certain I gasped out loud because that's not embarrassing at all. I wondered if the goddess Ivy mentioned was responsible for the male currently to be found in front of me. If so, I needed to know how to pray to her because she was owed some serious gratitude.

I didn't typically fawn over guys. That was just not me. But this guy was seriously droolworthy. I looked over his brown hair that was longer in the front and tousled over his forehead, a bit of scruff on his jaws, gorgeous glasses, and a box of books in his arms that he looked up from to lock his warm brown eyes with mine. Holy heck.

Was that drool? Oops.

"Hey, sorry. Am I interrupting?" my dream man asked, looking from Ivy to me.

Athena burst from Zeus's forehead, right? Did this guy just, *poof*, pop out of some part of my brain that visualized the perfect guy for me? That was the only logical explanation here.

Ivy didn't look up from the drawer she was digging in. "Hey, Nate. This is Elle. She's new to town and renting a space upstairs from me. Elle, this is Nate. He works at the library and has to dig through my deliveries to find the books he needs because that's where my life is right now. Poor guy, he probably got hives from looking at the chaos of the backroom. Ah, got them!" She looked up with an expression of triumph on her face. "Here you go, Elle."

I willed my body to move toward Ivy to grab the keys before fainting at Nate's feet or throwing myself at him. Either would probably be a bad look.

Nate glanced my way as he adjusted the box in his arms. "Welcome to Highland Falls, Elle."

"Thanks," I murmured, my face heating up because all of a sudden I was nervous and thirteen years old. And his forearms were doing things to me. What the heck? Forearms?

Ivy looked at a cell that was on the counter in front of her as it lit up. "Shoot. Emma's texting that I need to call her. Um, Nate, you know the apartments upstairs, right? Could you show Elle how to get up there? She's in number 2."

"Sure. I'll be back for the box, okay?" he asked as he placed the box in his arms on the counter.

"Yep. Flip the sign to Closed on your way out, but I won't lock up till you come back down. Elle, come in tomorrow. Hopefully, my life will have calmed down, and we can have tea and get to know each other." Ivy gave me a harried smile.

"Sounds good."

Nate gestured for me to go ahead of him, and I headed out the door.

He stepped out onto the street behind me. "Where's your car?"

I pointed at my Subaru.

"Want to take a load up as we go?"

Calm, Elle, calm. I cleared my throat and was thrilled when my voice didn't come out too creaky. "Sure. Ivy said the place is furnished, so I don't really have a lot."

Nate and I each grabbed a duffel bag, he got a box, and I grabbed a suitcase.

He led me to the exterior door that I assumed accessed the apartments, just between Pages and the store next door. There weren't a ton of stairs, but the staircase was sure steep. I wondered if going up and down it each day could count as a workout. Probably not, but they were no joke. My ass might thank me after a week or so. Or maybe not.

At the top on the small landing, Nate pointed toward the door with a two on it, and I let us in. We entered into the dining space with a round table. It was adjacent to a small sitting area with a love seat, chair, and coffee table. The kitchen was open with a pass-through to the dining area. There appeared to be a short hall with two doors. One had to be the bathroom and one the bedroom.

It was currently a blank canvas beyond the utilitarian furniture, but it was perfect.

I eased my load onto the table. Looking over to Nate, I gathered the courage to speak. "Thanks so much. You can leave that all here."

Nate put down his box, then looked around. "Good space. Is this bigger or smaller than where you were?"

I laughed without meaning to. "I was in downtown Chicago in a studio, so this is looking like I'm living large."

Nate nodded. "Well, I should let you go so you can get settled." He paused before opening the door. With a look back to me, he asked, "Do you need advice on restaurants for dinner? I'm guessing you don't have groceries yet."

"I have some staples in the boxes in my car." I glanced at my phone to see Ava had just replied that she was en route to help me unpack. "My sister is on her way to help. I'm guessing we'll order pizza."

"Giuseppe's," Nate said. "Best pizza in town." He looked unsure for a minute. "Not sure what you do or how much you like reading, but if you don't want to buy all your books, come to the Ryan Library. That's where I work, and it's a pretty special space."

"Yeah?" I asked. "What makes it special?" I patted myself on the back for continuing the conversation.

"Well, it's in an old house. Cool little nooks and stuff. And not to brag, but the people who work there are pretty nice too." He smoothed down his shirt, seemingly a little nervous.

My heart sped up a little bit. *Talk, Elle.*

"I work from home, so if you all don't mind people loitering, I might have to take you up on that."

Nate's eyes locked on mine. "Sounds like my favorite kind of people. Hope to see you there soon." His voice had a gravelly quality that I felt travel through my core.

Holy moly.

Looked like I'd be working from the library tomorrow.

2

———————————

LIGHTNING STRIKE

Nate

The front door shut behind me just as my phone vibrated from my pocket. Thinking of Elle, a feeling of excitement flooded me for a moment. That was crazy. I'd just met the woman and made the rookie mistake of not exchanging numbers. Maybe she'd actually follow through and I'd see her at the library soon. One could only hope.

I slid my phone out and made my way to my couch, dropping into it as I glanced down. The text message greeting me was from Chris, a former colleague at CPL, Chicago Public Library.

Chris: *I'm considering filing a missing person's report. Where the hell are you?*

Me: *Sorry. Didn't mean to drop off. You know how it can be in a new job.*

Chris: *What can possibly be so stressful down in southern Illinois? Someone's cow get loose?*

Me: *One, it's central Illinois and you know it. Southern Illinois doesn't begin until you hit the cross in Effingham.*

Two, yes. The Lietzes' cows did get loose last week. How'd you know? School buses rerouted and everything. Want to come down and help with traffic?

Chris: *Jesus, who are you and what are you doing down there? We're all headed to Kasey's tonight. You should come back up and visit. You're missed.*

I sank back in the couch, staring across the room as memories flitted through my mind. Months ago we would have headed to Kasey's Tavern after work. Danny would slide beers toward us across the bar, and the weight of the day would disappear. After a few, we might have gone for pizza or maybe a burger at Au Cheval. Our Chicago nights had been filled with laughter and colleagues that had become friends.

And I'd left it all behind.

Vibrations from my phone caused me to look down once again.

Chris: *Giving you shit, man. You know that, right?*

I shook my head and picked up my phone.

Me: *Yep, asshole. Kidding, kidding. Have a great time. We'll have to get together after the holiday.*

I watched to see if Chris would text again. Nothing. I sighed as I pulled myself up and headed through the living room to my bedroom, where the night stretched ahead of me.

My house had been my grandparents' place for as long as I could remember. When they left it to me after they passed, I'd been grateful. This place was a clear example of how lucky I was to grow up in the family I did. I didn't have siblings or cousins, but I had my parents and my grandparents. We were a close-knit group, and this was where we'd celebrated everything.

I loved Chicago. I made a hell of a lot more money up there, though it didn't go as far. But after the lawyer called to let me know that I'd been left this house, well, I felt like I'd been called home.

And I didn't regret it, I really didn't. I'd always loved Highland. I loved this place. My parents were closer here than they were to Chicago. Life was good.

If I was a little nervous, it wasn't that I thought I'd made the wrong choice by leaving it all behind. The library I'd moved to was great. The staff was a riot and made work fun. I wished I felt a bit more job security; it was such a small staff. And maybe once I sold my condo in a few months, my budget would breathe easier.

But it was all good.

As long as I ignored the feelings of something missing.

Tuesday morning dawned and I headed to work, listening to music in my headphones as I walked down the street. It was fascinating to think of the complete switch in my life in a few short months. In Chicago, I'd gotten to work via public transportation and walking. You walked fast and focused, not stopping to look around, but you got where you were going.

Here? I might not even pass a person—walking or driving—on the way to work. It was quiet, peaceful.

If anyone was on their porch, they'd say hello or wave. Heck, people might come out and talk to me, ask how my day was. Luckily it wasn't a complete culture shock, since I'd spent a lot of summers here, but it had been something to adjust to once again.

Jogging up the steps into the library, I breezed in the

door to see Emma and Gabby, both at the circulation desk at the front of the house. I didn't know the Ryan sisters who'd left their home to the town for use as the library—they passed long before I was in this world—but I appreciated their gift to Highland. This library was unique and homey. In other words, perfect.

"It's about time," Gabby complained.

I stopped and gave her a look. Gabby was one of my favorite coworkers and had zero filter, which made for interesting days. But I had no idea where she was going with this.

"What? I'm early."

She shook her head. "I need someone to save me from the real-life romance stories that are surrounding me right now."

I looked to Emma and raised a brow. She simply smiled serenely. Emma didn't get worked up about much.

"Aidan and Grace were here, and Gabby made a comment about too much PDA, though Aidan was just a bit handsy..."

"When isn't he? Though if I was Grace, I'd soak that in. The man is gorg," Gabby muttered. "And then there is your goliath."

I shook my head at the blatant jealousy from Gabby. Our boss, Grace, had the marriage you'd think you could only find in a work of fiction. And Max was our colleague Emma's fiancé. I'd met him several times over the past few months since I moved here. He seemed great, and we'd tried to make plans to get together for a drink, but his schedule had been crazy at Highland Woods, the state park outside town. He was working on a few new programs this year and had been buried in getting them off the ground.

"Max was here?" I asked.

"Is here." A deep voice came from the back. A few seconds later, Max appeared with a coffee mug that he handed Emma, who he proceeded to kiss, much to Gabby's dismay.

"See what I'm talking about?" She shook her head, but her grin belied her actual happiness that our friend and colleague had such a great guy.

Pulling back, Max looked my way. "Hey, Nate, what's your schedule look like this week? Drinks at Homestead?"

The library wasn't open very late, so my schedule was wide open with a whole lot of nothingness. "Open, you?"

"Thursday? Jake is smoking wings for a special at the brewery. He and Sully both said they'd be up to hang out too."

I wanted to laugh at how happy plans to meet up with some guys made me. Hell, I felt like a kid at a new school, grateful that I might have a friend.

"Thursday's great."

"Six sound good?"

"Yep."

Max gave Emma a kiss and headed out the door with a wave.

"I see how it is. You're ditching us in favor of hanging with the guys." Gabby picked up some books off the desk to reshelve.

"Gabs," Emma said, "be nice."

"Meeeeooooowwwww?"

I glanced down to see Gabby's cat, Aslan, wind her way through my legs.

"See, Aslan agrees, Emma. Not being mean." Gabby loaded up the cart and wheeled over toward the young adult section.

"It's fine, Nate." Emma placed a hand on my shoulder.

"Max has been looking forward to hanging out with you. And while Gabby enjoys teasing, we're all happy you're here and making yourself at home."

"Thanks, Emma." Between Emma and Grace, I really felt like I had two sisters looking out for me. Gabby would be the friend in class who got me in trouble for laughing behind the teacher's back, and to be honest, I needed them all. I realized that the heaviness that had weighed me down the night before had lessened. I did have people around me and was gaining even more. I just needed to remember that starting over took time.

I squeezed by Emma to sink down behind the desk and checked the computer, looking for requests we needed to fill for our patrons or the library loan system. I lost myself for a bit, scanning the screen, making lists, calling out to Gabby to grab books and straighten up the space. Before I knew it, over an hour had passed and the smell of coffee pervaded the space.

I pushed back from the desk, ready to turn and head toward the kitchen, when a patron by the window caught my eye.

Elle.

We had a smaller farm table set up as a workspace in the front room. Part of it was pushed against the window to allow for as much room as possible around it. People sat there to work, chat about books, and read. Today Elle sat, staring out the window, seemingly lost in thought.

It was ridiculous how happy I was at the sight of this woman I hadn't spoken to for more than ten minutes in my life, but there it was.

I moved over to her, but she was so zoned out she didn't register that I was there, so I cleared my throat.

Elle jumped and spun her head toward me.

Damn.

Here it was, ten in the morning the day after she moved to a new town. Her long brown hair was down and damp. I didn't know much about makeup, but she either wasn't wearing any or she knew how to make it look like that. Yesterday she'd worn clothes that Gabby would classify as stylish but casual. Today she was in a large cream sweatshirt that was so baggy it was rolled up by her hands, one of which she'd been using to twirl her hair.

"Nate," she whispered.

I grinned. "Do I sound full of myself if I say I'm glad you remembered me?"

Her face captivated me with a wide smile. "Not if I can say the same, or I guess I hoped you remember me too."

I snorted. As if I could forget her. "Elle, let me assure you now that I absolutely do remember you. Did you get settled in last night? And how was the pizza?"

Her laughter solidified something inside me, but hell if I knew what it was. "You were right, Giuseppe's is amazing."

"You shouldn't let any Chicagoans hear you say that. They don't think there can be good pizza south of I-80."

She laughed. "So true. And I heard the coffee place—I think Ava said it's called the Sanctuary—is good, but I didn't make it over this morning. Maybe tomorrow. I needed to get a jump on some work today and thought I'd check out your library." She looked around, then back to me. "You described this place perfectly. It is exactly what I need. Sometimes it's hard when you work at home. You can easily feel closed off from the world."

I considered Elle's words. I didn't work at home, but I did feel closed off from everything else of late. Hopefully, hanging out with Max and his friends would be a step in the right direction. Hell, I hoped Elle was part of my path forward as well. I was drawn to this woman in a way I couldn't explain. I wanted to date her, for certain. But more than that, I wanted to get to know her. I felt like something in me recognized something in her. Like I wanted to be her friend.

Where the hell had that come from?

"Well, our coffee isn't at the same level as the stuff Allyson has at the Sanctuary, but it's pretty good. Want me to get you a cup?"

Elle looked at me in surprise. "Really?"

"Black? Cream? Sugar?"

"Um, I usually put a splash of mocha creamer in."

"I've got a hot chocolate mix that a lot of us use for the same reason. I'll put some of that in. Be right back." I tapped her table and headed back toward the kitchen.

Walking through the nonfiction section, Gabby whispered to me as I passed, "Picking up dates at work now?"

"Shush."

In the kitchen, I grabbed a mug and mixed up a coffee for Elle. Just as I was turning to head back to her, my grandfather's voice popped into my head, clear as day.

The day I met your grandmother, Nathaniel, I felt like I'd been struck by lightning. Prettiest girl I ever did see, but somehow I knew—I just knew—she was going to be the best friend I'd ever had. Find your best friend, and you will have found the one. That's all you need. Man alive, I loved that woman something fierce.

I looked at the back of Elle, who was lost in thought at the window again.

Oh boy.

3

REDS OF CHRISTMAS

SIX WEEKS LATER

Elle

The cursor on my computer blinked, taunting me. The words just didn't want to come.

Shit.

I dropped my head to the table, wondering if pounding it repeatedly would be a good look.

Probably not.

"Elle, your head is far too pretty to bruise in this way. How can I help?"

I groaned. Great. Now I not only looked like a fool, I was doing it in front of Nate. That seemed on brand for my day.

I slowly looked up, willing someone to call him away. No dice. He stood there, looking stupidly amazing. Hot book nerd all the way. Mussed hair, gorgeous glasses, a bit of stubble, fitted button-down rolled up and showcasing those forearms that I'd somehow developed an obsession with. Check, check, and check.

Hell, checkmate. How did I spin this one? Nate fortunately took pity on me as he dropped into the chair next to me and tapped my computer screen.

"Work-work or dream-work?"

"I'm sorry?"

"Are you working on your day job or your dream novel?"

"Shhhhhhhh," I said, glancing around to see who was near.

He shook his head as I worked not to panic. "Elle, why is this such a big secret?"

I groaned, burying my face in my arms. "Ava doesn't even know."

"Your sister doesn't know you want to write a book, but you told me? Why?"

Well, that was the million-dollar question, wasn't it?

"Have you emailed that agent back yet?"

I groaned into my arms, regretting the fact that I not only told Nate about my secret novelist dream, but that an agent I met was interested in pitching my book when I got at least three-quarters of it written. He must have put some type of truth serum in my coffee that day. It was the only answer for my loose lips.

Over the past six weeks in Highland, I'd developed a routine. Nights were taken up with Ava, rotating dinners with my new neighbors, Nic and Kate, and some girls' nights out with them, my sister, or a combination of people I'd met between the bookstore and the library. My social life was far fuller than it'd been in Chicago but still relaxed and quiet, which was just as I liked it.

My days also had structure. Mornings found me up early to take yoga from Kristine's rotating location of yoga classes. Though this week she'd finally opened her studio next to the bookstore, which was amazing. After yoga I typically got coffee at the Sanctuary and headed to the library or went straight to the library to get coffee here. The Sanctuary was an adorable café, and I could easily have worked there. So what drew me to the library again and again?

Nate Roberts.

Jesus. I had it bad for this guy. Over the past six weeks, I'd sat here, soaking in any attention he shot my way. If it was only that the man was gorgeous, I would have let this little crush go months ago. But that wasn't it. Nate was gorgeous *and* funny *and* kind *and* considerate.

And I'd told him my long-held secret dream.

Ahhhhhhhh.

Picking my head up, I saw a coffee mug had somehow appeared in front of me. I glanced from the mug to Nate. "You brought me coffee?"

"Yep. You were too busy having a meltdown to notice. It's okay, I forgive you." He sat back, the picture of ease.

I glanced at the mug. It looked like he'd added the perfect amount of hot chocolate mix, exactly the way I liked it. I mean, seriously, who knew there were guys like this out in the world?

Or maybe not guys plural. Maybe it was just Nate. Surely if he wasn't an anomaly, people would be talking.

More to the point, how in the hell didn't he have a girlfriend?

Yep, there went the old pang to the heart. Super.

"You're avoiding the question, Ms. Robinson. Your sister doesn't know about Peter?"

I doubled down on the "shhhhhh" this time.

Nate's grin was Cheshire cat–worthy. "So, Elle, what you're saying is that you don't want me telling people about Peter and Thea, who find a body in the catacombs of Paris in the twenties? That's what I shouldn't be talking about."

Head to table. Wave the white flag. I was done, thank you very much.

I felt Nate push back the chair at my side and stand up. Then I felt hot air from his mouth near my ear.

Shiver.

"Your secret is safe with me, Elle. But I think you should own this dream. Your writing is too good to ignore it."

With that, he walked away. Hopefully he hadn't noticed the goose bumps that had risen in response to his proximity—or the hitch in my breath.

Yep. Nothing to see here. Nothing at all.

I ran my hand over the hangers in front of me at my closet again. It didn't seem to matter. I'd scanned my wardrobe several times, and nothing was saying wear me!

I dropped dramatically to my bed and grabbed my phone.

Me: *I have nothing to wear.*

Ava's response was immediate.

Ava: *Oh good, insecurity right on schedule then?*

Me: *Can't you come tonight?*

Ava: *Sorry, babe. School holiday party and I planned it. Ivy's going with you. Relax and enjoy.*

Ava: *And red suede jacket, black knee-length, body-hugging LBD, and some kick-ass shoes. You've got this.*

With a sigh, I begrudgingly got up and grabbed the clothes Ava had mentioned. She was right, it would work. How she could pick the perfect outfit without even seeing my closet was a mystery for the ages.

After a quick change, I looked in the mirror and felt pretty good about the reflection looking back at me. Taking a quick picture, I shot off a text to Ava and got a thumbs-up back in return. Noting the time, I moved to my couch to kill a few minutes until Ivy would be ready.

Clicking on a social media app, I opened up the memories from that day. I flipped through some, realizing how distant my time in Chicago seemed. I'd had a few friends, to be certain, but so many of my posts in the past few years were from me on my own.

Finally I hit a picture from four years ago. I'd been in Chicago at my job for a few months, and I was headed out to a Christmas party. I could see my nerves from the way I bit my lower lip, but I'd posted the pic I'd taken with one of the other editors, Julie. She was tiny, below five foot, slender. I didn't tend to feel tall around people, but Julie had made me feel like I was far more than four or five inches above her. I also easily outweighed her by sixty pounds. That night? I hadn't cared. In my fitted green sweater dress, I'd felt curvy, sexy.

My stomach thudded as I remembered the comments. Telling myself I shouldn't, I still clicked. Most, if I was looking at them without bias, said I looked gorgeous and wished me a happy holiday. Several girls from college, however, made passive-aggressive comments about the need for moderation during the holidays. Cautioning me that I shouldn't *let myself go*.

Why did women do this to each other?

Ava had taken them to task, and while I wanted to say their comments didn't pierce the armor I'd worked to put up, they had.

I blinked back tears. I'd pulled back from social media after that. Hell, to be honest, I'd pulled back from a lot more. I'd dated casually in Chicago but kept everything light. A date here and there but nothing deep. I'd promised myself that I wasn't going to be in a position to get hurt again. It was too much vulnerability for me. No, thanks. Over the past four years, I'd worked on myself, worked to retrain the way my brain reacted. I was stronger than I was in the past, but I was also human.

I glanced down at my fitted dress and was pissed at my immediate worry that I should change. Enough.

Ava would kick my ass if she heard my thoughts right now. I looked good.

A knock at the door pulled me out of my tiny pity party. It was time to go.

Ivy and I entered the brewery, weaving through tables as she made a beeline for a guy that I assumed was Jake, her fiancé. Right before we reached him, I felt a tug on my arm. I turned to see a person from my yoga class and quickly greeted her before catching up with Ivy.

Jake was gorgeous, clearly. Ivy had talked about the man nonstop anytime I'd seen her over the past month. They'd had a rocky go at one point, but if the way they were looking at each other was any indication, their relationship was full steam ahead. My God, I worried we all might be incinerated simply by being in their presence.

I hadn't met Jake, though he often visited Ivy at the bookstore. We seemed to always just miss each other, so I'd looked forward to getting to know the guy that had captured my friend's heart.

Ivy introduced us, and Jake went to grab us all beer. Tonight businesses all over town were celebrating the holidays with this ticketed event called the Reds of Christmas. Ivy had red velvet cupcakes available at the bookstore that Nic was passing out. I think Kristine was giving out peppermint-scented cooldown towels at the yoga studio. Ivy had said we could head around the square and check out the other stores, but the brewery felt like enough for me.

I thanked Jake for my beer and felt suddenly self-conscious, like there were eyes on me. I turned to scan the crowd, and my eyes locked on Nate's.

His gaze on mine made my insides heat up until I was certain my face was the color of my jacket. He started to smile and take a step toward me, so I did the only thing that made any sense.

I fled to the bathroom.

4
____

THE FATES

Nate

Gabby walked into the kitchen at the library with a knowing grin on her face. "Guess who's here?" she said in a singsong voice.

"Gabs...," I warned, working to concentrate on stirring my coffee.

"Oh, Nate. Let's stop playing the game where you try to deny that you've been low-key flirting with one Ms. Elle Robinson for the past six weeks. Heck, Tim has a pool going with Lou as to when either of you are going to get the balls to finally do something about it."

"A pool?"

"Yep. I've got Christmas, so I need you to move as slow as you have been for the next two and a half-ish weeks. Cool? Cool."

Gabby danced around the large farm table we had in the middle of the kitchen. It often functioned as a spot for staff meetings; however, this place was relaxed enough that we let patrons use it for book clubs too.

I ignored her and took a sip of my coffee, moving to the windows that looked out on the backyard.

Getting on Tim and Lou's radar was not high on my list of things to do. Tim was a part-time employee here at the library but was moving to full time next week, which brought me a sense of relief.

Every day I was more and more convinced that leaving Chicago had been the right call. The only thing not putting me completely at ease would be the need to unload my condo and job security. Joining the staff of a library that only had two full-time employees, I'd stressed that my added position might be on the chopping block if city finances took a turn. Instead, they were now increasing Tim's position as the city had decided to invest more in the library. None of the part-time employees had wanted to move to full time when I came on, but now Tim had decided to dive in. I was feeling more secure in this position by the day.

At any rate, Tim was hard to describe. It felt like he could step out from the pages of a rom-com: flamboyant, outspoken, and hilarious. Add to that Lou, a seventysome-thing busybody who somehow knew everything that was going on in town. I feared I might not have as low a profile as I thought I did.

"When did this pool start?" I asked, looking out the window. I worked to keep the tone of my voice almost offhand. Gabs didn't need to know this was actually concerning me.

"About five seconds after you and Elle gave each other the fuck-me eyes at the Reds of Christmas on Friday night." Gabby positively cackled as she moved to the coffee maker to pour her own cup.

I calmly took another drink, though I was feeling

anything but chill. Elle had run after taking in those fuck-me eyes I shot her way on Friday night. I didn't need her getting wind of these busybodies.

Behind me, I heard more footsteps as someone else entered the kitchen.

"Nate, did you see that Elle is here?"

It was Emma. I let my head thud to the glass in response. Jesus. These women.

"What's wrong with him?" She asked Gabby in a hushed voice.

"I told him about Tim's pool."

"Oh."

Long pause from Emma. She was sweet. Maybe she was debating how to break it to Gabby and Tim that a pool on when two people might get together was not needed.

Emma cleared her throat. "Nate, I have December 15, so maybe you could go chat with Elle?"

What was wrong with these people? I lightly tapped my head against the window, wondering if it would knock some sense into me or wake me up from this fever dream.

"What's going on here?"

Terrific. Enter Grace, the director of our library.

"Nate seems stressed about Tim's pool." Emma volunteered up. Bless her heart, as my grandma would say.

"Well, that's not okay," Grace began.

Thank goodness. She was going to be the voice of reason with these coworkers of ours.

"Because I have the eleventh. I need you to shit or get off the pot, Nate," Grace announced.

Yep. This is what I got for working in a small town. My fault, really. After growing up in a neighboring town, as well as visiting my grandparents here, I really had known better.

Maybe I should revisit that whole glad-I-left-Chicago mindset from a few minutes ago?

I turned to look at these three ladies across the kitchen as they stood watching me with a fair share of amusement evident.

"Where's your string?" I asked.

Grace tipped her head to the side. "What?"

I gestured to encompass them all. "Which one of you is Atropos? You know, you're the Fates, right? You're screwing with my destiny here, aren't you? That's what's happening."

Grace shook her head as she headed to the coffee maker. "Enough on the Greek mythology, Nathaniel. Now, we are the gender of your intended. Want to bounce any ideas off us? We're here to help. Should we role play?"

"But not too quickly. Maybe ease in?" Emma commented.

"Agreed. Take your time," Gabby said with an easy smile.

"Enough," I growled and opened a cabinet. Was there anything to eat? I hadn't replenished my snacks this week. Damn. I began straightening the crap on the counters.

"Okay, ladies. Let's go easy on Nate. He's stress cleaning." Grace looked at the other two, then to me. "Switching topics, have you unloaded your place in Chicago yet?"

Ugh. Were they mind readers now? Just the comment from Grace made me want to rub my temples. Was that a headache coming on?

I moved my coffee over on the counter before hopping up. "Not yet. The subletter will be officially moving on at the first of the year. I need to write up a listing, but I'm hoping to recoup not only what I bought the place for, but the improvements I made." I thought through everything I needed to get done and felt more than a bit overwhelmed. "I want to look over the listing again and check around at what similar properties are being priced at to make sure I'm in line with the rest of the market. I just haven't made it a priority."

"You should have Elle help you," Gabby piped up.

I gave her a look, the meddling busybody that she was.

She raised her hands. "No, this isn't about that. Promise. Just saying she helped me write up some sale posts for crap I'd bought Aslan when I first got her, but she hadn't liked. For example, the giant climbing tower that was taking up a good portion of my living room. Aslan just looked at it with disgust."

This was not shocking at all. Gabby's cat had definite opinions and didn't hesitate to share them. Circling back. "Elle helped you?"

Gabby gave me a mischievous smile. "Yep, sure did. She said it's similar to what she does for work, and she's good at it. I was even able to sell the tower for a bit more than I bought it for."

I moved to the doorway that took you from the kitchen and peeked into the library. Sure enough, the focus of our conversation sat at the table in the front room by the window. She stretched her back, tilted her head to the side. Her long brown hair cascaded over her shoulder. Spending time with her almost daily over the past six weeks had only reinforced my gut reaction when we first met. Elle had become my friend, and I was on board for a whole lot more.

I'd thought about approaching her the other night at the Reds event, but her dash to the bathroom made me worry. I didn't think these feelings were one-sided, but I sure didn't want to scare her off. Maybe this was just the inroad I needed.

5

___

DEATH BY TEXT MESSAGE

Elle

I pushed my laptop back and stretched my neck to the right, then left. The satisfying pop resounded in the quiet nook of the library. For a Monday afternoon, there weren't many patrons milling around. Looking out the window, I noted the damp leaves on the ground were partially covered with a dusting of snow. We'd had an interesting start to winter in my new town, early snowfalls in November, but no real accumulation yet in December. Frankly, I was grateful for the return of sweater weather.

Bringing my attention back to the library, I saw Nate coming out of the kitchen. My cheeks heated. What did I even say to him after my almost comical repeated avoidance on Friday night? There was no explaining it. Tugging my laptop back toward me, I worked to look busy while watching Nate out of the corner of my eye. From my spot at the table in front of the windows, I could see the circulation desk where he was helping a teen who had been waiting to check out.

I glanced at the cover of the top book in the teen's hand.

Excellent choice. I'd read *Aristotle and Dante Discover the Secrets of the Universe* years ago based on Ava's recommendation. Her job teaching high school English resulted in a never-ending list of books for me to read.

Vibrations from my phone pulled me back to the present. *Speak of the devil*, I thought as Ava's name flashed up. Quickly I tapped to open the text.

Ava: *Hey stranger, you coming over tonight? Dinner?*

Ava: *I mean, you moved to town and I barely see you. I'm beginning to forget what you look like.*

Me: *Overreact much? I saw you a few days ago for coffee.*

Ava: *Too many days ago, my sweets. That's too long. I spend my days with seventeen-year-olds who believe they are the center of the universe. I need to see my little sis. That's why you moved here after all. Right? Come over.*

Me: *Working now. Maybe later?*

Ava: *Working where...*

Me: *...*

Ava: *You're at the library again. Right?*

Ava: *For God's sake, Elle, ask the guy out.*

Me: *If he wanted to ask me out, he would have. I don't need to embarrass myself.*

Ava: *Grow a pair, baby sis. One, how would he ask you out? From what you said, you run away from him when he has the chance. And, I'll note, you've talked about nothing but that glorious hunk of man since moving here six weeks ago. I asked around, he's unattached—*

Me: *YOU ASKED AROUND?*

Ava: *Shh. You're in a library.*

Ava: *So, is he as beautiful as ever?*

I glanced over at Nate to see that he was looking over a

stack of books on the front desk, typing something into the computer. I took in the tousled brown hair to the stubble on his jaw to the Henley that stretched across his lean chest to his jeans that cupped what I knew from advanced study was a glorious ass. Yeah, you could say he wasn't a chore to observe.

My phone vibrated again.

Ava: *Well...*

Me: *Out of my league.*

Ava: *Shut up.*

Ava: *Clearly I need to come down and kick your ass. You are gorgeous.*

I grinned at her reply. *Ava* was gorgeous. And I'd worked a hell of a lot on my self-image not to play the comparison game against anyone, including my sis, not that she was about that. However, Ava's wavy brown hair, long lean legs, killer ass, and breasts to die for, tended to be what our screwed-up society elevated. Ava took after our dad in height. I was a mirror image of our mom.

Long thick brown hair, freckles, an hourglass figure that on someone taller than my whopping height of five foot three would've been gentle curves. For me, I heard a lot of *baby got back* in middle school. Thanks, Sir Mix-a-Lot. Grateful you liked those big butts.

As I grabbed my phone to reply to Ava, I jumped after hearing a throat being cleared. Looking up, I saw faded jeans, then a forest green Henley, then Nate's beautiful face.

"Sorry to startle you," he said, his eyes gleaming. "You look lost in thought over here, Ms. Robinson. Anything you need?" He slid a coffee cup next to my computer, perfectly made, as usual.

"One, thank you. Two, *Elle*." I said, taking a sip and sighing with enjoyment. Today he had also somehow added a peppermint flavor. Perfection.

Nate grinned, his eyes dancing with amusement. "One, you're welcome. And two, I know, *Elle*. Just teasing. Anything else you need?"

I couldn't help it. I felt a tremble sweep through me. All the folks that worked here knew me by name, but the way that Nate said it, mmmm. It warmed me up.

"Elle?"

I looked back to see Nate watching me with a touch of concern. Good grief, must have zoned out there for a minute.

"What?"

With a bit of smirk, Nate said, "Just checking to see if you needed anything."

"No..." I wanted to groan out loud. I sounded breathless, like I'd just run a race. I'd frequently asked myself what the heck was wrong with me over the past six weeks. Somehow the presence of this man reduced me to a quivering mess. He smelled of soap and the outdoors, and all I ever wanted to do was bury my face in his chest and soak it in.

Chill, Elle.

"You have fun at the brewery on Friday?" he asked.

"Yep." I patted myself on the back for my stronger voice. "You?"

Nate gave me a warm look. "Sure did. Would have had even more fun if I got a chance to talk to you."

My phone vibrated its siren call from the table, causing us to glance down. A reprieve. I saw Ava's name flash on the screen.

Glancing back to Nate, I whispered, "Sorry, it's my sister."

Nate looked down as the phone lit up again, paused, then grinned. "I'll let you get to it. You know where I am if you need anything."

Mutely, I nodded and looked to my phone, already feeling the loss of a guy that wasn't even mine. Those feelings vanished when I saw the text that was currently lighting up the screen from Ava.

Ava: *Saddle up, Elle. I'm sure Mr. Nate Roberts would be perfectly fine with you jumping his bones. Get it, girl. Come over when you're done. Love you!*

I gasped.

Holy.

Shit.

I was dead. Right? Surely, I was.

Maybe he hadn't seen that message. Had all of it been visible on the phone? Feeling my cheeks flush, I slowly moved to look up, praying he wouldn't be there.

Yep, still standing there, book in hand, watching.

Fabulous.

As our gazes locked, Nate took a step closer, his scent surrounding me as I prayed to be swallowed into the floor. He laid the book down and braced himself on the table.

Even while swimming in mortification, I noted those enticing forearms. In my steady diet of romance books, they often waxed poetic about forearms, which had always puzzled me. Who gave a damn about forearms? Looks like I just hadn't been around the right guys, because Nate's forearms did something to me.

Nate proceeded to rock my world as he leaned down to whisper in my ear. "FYI, your sister's plan sounds good to me."

Standing up, he shot me a wink and then headed across the room to meet Gabby, who was coming down from the offices upstairs.

I worked to even out my breathing and find a way to ignore the urge telling me to drop my head to the table and give up the ghost.

Seriously?

Ava and her timing could not possibly be worse. Allowing for another quick glance in his direction, I found Nate watching from where he now stood with Gabby as she sorted a cart of books into piles.

His eyes heated and he raised an eyebrow at me.

Whoa. What the hell was going on?

6

THE SHIT HITS THE FAN

Nate

Gabby was dancing again, this time around the circulation desk as she sorted books from the cart into two stacks—yes and no. The GSA at the local high school was holding a book club this month at their group meetings. One of the teachers had reached out to Grace to brainstorm a list of young adult books featuring LGBTQIA characters. I watched Gabby tap her chin on the spine of a book as she looked back and forth between the two piles.

"What's up, Gabs?"

She paused, mid tap. "I'm debating the merits of *Every Day* by David Leviathan. I mean the main character, *A*, doesn't really have a gender. Instead, every day they wake up in a new body. I'm not sure it would fit in this list we're creating."

I considered the book for a moment. "Well, it likely depends on what they want this list to accomplish." Gesturing at the book in her hands, I continued, "That one would certainly be a good jumping-off point for conversations on gender identity, being gender-fluid, et cetera."

Gabby nodded. "You're absolutely right." Dropping the book on her yes stack, she jerked her head toward Elle with a smirk. "Did you ask her to help with your listing?"

I looked back to Elle, who still had a flush spreading over her cheeks. "Not yet." I hesitated, wondering if I should share. Hell, what did I have to lose. Clearly I wasn't getting anywhere so far.

I jerked my head back in the direction of the kitchen, figuring it'd give us some privacy. Gabby followed me without a word.

That changed as soon as we entered. "What's with the change in venue, Roberts?"

Looking back toward the main library and seeing that no one was near, I looked at Gabby. "I saw a text on her phone."

Gabby's brows drew together. "Whose phone? Elle's?"

"Who do you think we are talking about here, Gabby?"

She rolled her eyes. "Continue, Mr. Snoops-a-lot."

"Not snooping, saw it accidentally when I glanced down. Elle said she was texting with her sister. The text that I saw on her phone said something about how she should jump my bones." I couldn't hold back the grin that popped up at the thought of seeing my name on Elle's phone, much less the content of the message. Elle jumping me? Where should I sign up?

"See," Gabby hissed. "This is not an unrequited attraction here, Nate. You need to ask her out."

I shook my head in disagreement. "I gave her a bit of an opening, and she didn't bite, Gabs. She can be shy. I don't want to scare her off."

Gabby looked skeptical. "Tell me more about this *opening* you supposedly gave her."

My body practically hummed with energy as I thought

back to Elle's cheeks flushing at my words, highlighting her freckles. God, she was sexy. Those curves didn't hurt. But damn, I loved talking to her too. While shy at times, she seemed comfortable with who she was. It was damn attractive.

Leaning out of the kitchen, I looked past the shelves of nonfiction books to see Elle's back as she typed away. She paused, leaning her head on her hand as she twirled some hair around a finger before resuming her typing. Watching her, I wondered what it was that she was working on today.

"Editing," Gabby whispered from over my shoulder.

Looking down, I found Gabby standing right beside me, watching Elle as well.

"Excuse me?"

"You asked what she was always working on."

"I asked that out loud?"

Gabby grinned at me as she bumped my hip with hers. "Sure did, big guy. And what have you been doing for the past month that you didn't know Elle's job?"

I didn't answer, not because I didn't know what Elle did, but because I knew how much trust Elle had put in me to share her dream. For her, I prayed she was writing about Peter, Thea, and some crazy mystery in the Parisian catacombs. I wanted her to write that novel and surprise everyone with how amazing it was, including herself.

Hell, each time she'd come in to write over the past month and a half, I'd warn myself not just to sit and watch her like some creeper. She'd twirl her hair while typing, occasionally wrinkling her nose that had freckles scattered across. Thinking back, I could picture her head nodding in time to whatever music was flowing through her earbuds. And then there was the first time she stood up and I saw those curves in yoga pants and a thin T-shirt.

Holy shit.

I'd been grateful that I was sitting at the desk because my body reacted as if I was still a teen who couldn't control his reactions rather than a man in my late twenties. Damn.

"Earth to Nate," Gabby called.

Not pulling my eyes off Elle, I merely mumbled, "What?"

Gabby chuckled before tugging me back into the kitchen. "Let's make a plan, my friend. We need to get you this girl. Let's go."

I pulled back as Gabby grabbed my arm and tugged me forward. "Gabs." I tried to stall.

"Nope. Even if it means I lose this pool, we need to get you at least at the starting line."

"I am at the starting line. Hell, I'm past it. We just don't need to make it a sprint." I sputtered as we passed through the nonfiction section and were only steps from Elle's table.

Gabby gave me a look of derision. "Six weeks, Nate. *Six. Weeks.*"

At this point, we were right by Elle's table. Elle looked up and saw Gabby and me, her cheeks flushing.

She tilted her head as she looked between the two of us, her brows drawing together. "Hey, guys. Do you need something?"

I had a strong desire to sweep her up in my arms and hold her. That was new. Thank God Gabby couldn't read my mind. I hoped Grace and Emma didn't come down from the offices above. That would make this even more of a circus than it already was.

"I was telling Nate how you helped me write the listing for Aslan's unused toys and mentioned that you might be able to help him out," Gabby said, giving me a nudge.

Elle straightened in her seat as she looked to me, her

face clearing. "What do you need to sell? I can absolutely help."

Gabby gave me a nod and moved away as I pulled out the chair across from Elle. Okay, maybe this hadn't been Gabs's worst idea yet.

"I've been holding on to my place up in Chicago, kind of as insurance to make sure everything worked out down here. But it's going to be available at the start of the year, and I don't want to deal with renting it out anymore."

Elle nodded as she pulled up something on her computer. "Okay, what's the address? We could look to see what the comps are. And do you have any pictures of your place? Then I can get an idea on what to write in the ad."

Her brow furrowed as her phone and computer both pinged. She scanned something and her eyes widened as she took a quick intake of breath.

Her fingers were flying.

"Elle? Is everything okay?"

Her head shook briefly in the negative as she murmured, "Hold on a second."

I watched as her fingers furiously tapped on her phone, opening an app, scanning, switching to another account, only to open another app.

"Shit," she muttered.

"What is it?" My gut clenched in concern.

"Umm, I'm not sure." She spun her computer to show me the screen.

It took a minute to take in. There was a photo of Elle and two other people. It looked like they were at some type of conference. Elle was wearing a dress I'd pay good money to see her in. It had a shit ton of cleavage and hugged every one of her curves.

Scanning the page, I saw that this was the social media

account for the education publisher that Elle worked for. Scrolling, I landed on the comments below the image. The first one was something about one of the people besides Elle in the picture. The next one made me growl.

Love every PD book these two have written. And that's a gorgeous dress on the other lady, but she needs a friend to dish on what's best for those curves. Not a great choice for a bigger gal. Whoa!

What the literal fuck? I looked at Elle.

She gave me a look. "I'm guessing you've only read the first few comments. I could give a lesser shit about what people think about the clothing I choose to put on my body. Keep reading."

I looked from her back to the screen. These comments hadn't bothered her, so what was it?

Halfway down the page, I found out.

7

SOCIAL MEDIA DUMPSTER FIRE

Elle

My stomach wouldn't stop clenching as I scanned down more of the comments as Nate scrolled. Honestly, the comment about my curves had given me some pause and pissed me off, but then I read on to find out why my boss, Sue, was upset. The text from Sue had simply included the link and the note to call. Clicking on the link made the bottom drop out of my orderly life.

I worked for the education company Smithfield, a publisher for professional development books for educators. I also did the copy for their catalog and worked closely with some of their author/educators. Two of their most well-known authors were who I was pictured with in the image Nate was looking at.

The two educators had written books and presented together for over fifteen years. They knew their shit and were pretty easy to work with on the books I'd edited for them. The photo was at a big teaching conference this past summer where I'd celebrated my fifth year with the company. And if we could believe the world of social media, one of the two was a blatant racist.

I'd never had that feeling from him, but I didn't know what these comments were in regard to. My first thought was to find what was being talked about online and where this happened, but I didn't know if I wanted to disappear down that problematic rabbit hole.

I texted my boss.

Me: *What's going on? Is this true?*

Sue: *We're looking into it. Did you see all the comments?*

Me: *On the social media post from last summer? I haven't read them all yet.*

Sue: *You're tagged in the picture. I'd stay off Twitter for a bit.*

Me: *What the hell? I haven't said anything.*

Sue: *I know, you just don't want to be brought into this by association. Just sit back while we sort through what was actually said.*

Me: *So you think there is truth to the accusation?*

Sue: *Let's say there's concern. I'll get back to you.*

I dropped my head into my hands, having zero energy to devote to this shitstorm.

"Elle," Nate's voice was low. "You okay?"

"Nope." I picked my head up because what else was there to do? "My boss says to stay off social media while they sort this all out." I gestured to the image still on my computer screen. "They have a book coming out next week that I worked on. Not sure if that will be impacted or not."

Nate studied me for a minute. "Want some more coffee?"

Dang, this guy got better and better. "Yes please."

"You need decaf in the afternoon?"

"Heck no, fully loaded please."

He nodded, then knocked on the table before getting up to head back to the kitchen. I watched him walk away and wondered if I could follow Ava's advice and ask him out. While I was more confident than I used to be, the comment on the picture today showed me that my armor wasn't bullet proof. I still felt the ding. And after six weeks, I had a feeling Nate could do far more damage than an offhand comment from a random asshole online. However, I was so tired of being alone. It was start dating or get serious about being a plant owner.

The bell over the front door pulled me out of my thoughts. Glancing to the front, I felt tension wash through me as my sister's mischievous grin met my gaze. What in the ever-loving hell?

"Ava," I hissed. "What are you doing here?"

Ava sauntered toward the table, glancing around as she got closer. "Well, where is he?"

My eyes rolled of their own accord. "Are you *serious?* There is zero reason for you to be here. You need a hobby."

Plopping in the chair Nate had recently vacated, Ava grinned. "Baby sister, you are my hobby. Besides, I have a reason to be here beyond getting you some action."

I didn't like the devilish glint I saw shining back at me. "What are you talking about?"

Gabby chose that moment to come out of the kitchen, coffee mug in hand. "Hey, sorry we weren't manning the store. Coffee waits for no one, you know?" She looked to Ava. "Hey, Ava, are you here for the book list? It's not quite finished, but I'd be glad to go over what we have so far."

My eyebrows drew together as I gave Ava one of my patented glares, learned from our mom. "What book list?"

Gabby glanced from me to Ava. "We've been pulling some books for the high school's GSA book club, and we're going to go over the titles with her later this week."

I raised a brow at my dear old sis, wanting to call bullshit. Nope, I wanted to scream it. There was no way that Ava just randomly reached out to the library for help with a book list. Beyond the fact that her school had a librarian, Ava devoured books. She could make a book list on her own in minutes. I had a strong feeling that she wanted to spend time at the Ryan Library and learn a bit more about one Nate Roberts. Meddling sisters.

"Umm, Ava, can I talk to you for a minute?" I ground out.

The wattage on Ava's grin increased exponentially. "Sorry, sis. I was swinging by to tell you that I had an appointment that I forgot about tonight and couldn't do dinner."

Ava's gaze found Nate headed from the kitchen toward our table with coffee, then she looked at me, tilting her head like she was considering something. "Say, crazy idea here. Since I bailed on your dinner plans, maybe you could meet up with Gabby and"—she gestured to Nate as he put the coffee in front of me—"Nate, is it? You all could have dinner instead. They can share the titles they were thinking of with you. We can talk about them later, and I can get your input. Sound good?" Ava stood up, looking like she was going to make a fast exit.

Before I could say *not so fast*, Gabby began nodding as she tapped her chin absentmindedly. "Great idea, Ava." She looked over her shoulder at Nate. "Nate, I have that *thing* tonight. Do you mind getting Elle up to speed on the books we were thinking about? If we have a core group of titles that we want to go forward with, I can request as many copies as we need through the interlibrary loan website and have them for you by the end of this week or beginning of next."

Nate looked completely confused. I'd feel bad for him if I wasn't so pissed at my meddling sister right now. What the literal fuck? Ava was clearly setting us up, and somehow Gabby had become her sidekick?

I interrupted Ava's reply to Gabby with a terse, "One, manners. Nate, Ava. Ava, Nate. Two, Ava. Porch. Now." Without looking back, I stormed out.

The sound of the front door closing behind me made me whirl around to see Ava moving across the porch with a wide grin stretched across her face. I snipped, "What the hell was that?"

"Tsk-tsk, Elle-belle. Where is the gratitude?"

"Gratitude? What do you think you're doing here?"

Ava looked to the heavens like she couldn't even remotely understand me. "Um, setting you up? Come on, that guy is dreamy. You can thank me later."

"Arrrggghhhh!" I threw my arms up in frustration and began to pace to the edge of the porch and back, taking a moment to appreciate the sweet little neighborhood and the traces of snow covering some of the ground. It wasn't exactly warm. We were going to need to wrap this up because I didn't have a coat out here like Ava. "Why are you insisting on interfering in my life?"

Leaning back against the porch railing, Ava watched me with a wary gaze. "I wouldn't need to interfere if you'd get to work. You will be old and gray before you ever make a move on the hot librarian in there, and you know it. I don't want you to end up with a houseful of cats, Elle. You deserve that guy. You've talked about nothing less for the past month."

I ran my hands through my hair. "There is so much to work with here I don't even know where to start. One, I would have made a move in time if I felt like it. Two, cats are cute, but I've decided I'm more of a houseplant person. And three, what's up with asking them for book lists? I know damn well you didn't need help with that—"

Ava raised her hand. "Actually, I did. I mean, I wanted to bring the public library in as partners in these book groups because I want the kids to see that more people care about them in town than a few teachers at the high school."

I paused, considering that. "Okay, that's not a terrible idea."

"I know. And also, might I add, you are full of shit. You've had six weeks and are still working to get up the nerve. I'm just giving you a push."

"It doesn't matter anyway."

"Why? Because he couldn't possibly be attracted to you or some other bullshit nonsense you have in your head? Get over yourself, Elle. You're gorgeous, funny, loyal, and any guy would be lucky to get a chance at you." Ava looked pissed.

"This isn't the me of my high school days, I do like who I am now. But you're sweet, Av, thanks."

"Of course," Ava dismissed. "You do the same for me. But quit stalling. Why haven't you made a move?"

"Many reasons," I said as I looked to the porch's ceiling. "Today's top ones include that it's been a shitty day with work, and I have no idea if he's even interested. Well, he indicated he might be, but I don't know if he was just trying to save me from embarrassment. Hell, maybe there's something going on with him and Gabby. He might not even be available." My stomach dropped, even as I said the words. God, it wasn't like anything had happened between us over the past month, just great conversations and a gut attraction that wouldn't leave.

"Um, excuse me. Not meaning to eavesdrop here, but I did anyway..." Gabby had stuck her head out of the library, and a wide grin stretched across her face. "Nate and I are just friends, if that's of any interest to you. He's like my big brother, so eww." Gabby scrunched her nose as she laughed, then wagged her eyebrows. "So just saying, if you're wanting to jump a certain hot librarian, I am happy to cheer you on. Might I suggest tonight's dinner as an excellent starting point?"

Good Lord, could this day get any worse? Of course the universe decided to answer just then, and the answer would be yes. Yes, it could.

"Ahem, excuse me." Nate stepped around Gabby to join the group on the porch, otherwise known as my current circle of hell. "One, just saying, if the hot librarian is in reference to me, thanks. Two, Elle, how about that dinner?" Nate was giving me a look I couldn't read, but holy hell, it made my lady parts, as Ava would say, take notice. Embarrassment and arousal were warring internally, and I had no idea which side would win.

"Um, this is a bit mortifying."

Ava knocked her shoulder into mine. "What my sister means to say is yes, dinner sounds great." Ava squeezed my arm as she moved from the porch railing to the door. "Gabby, do you still have those books on hold for me?"

Gabby slid inside after Ava, her voice floating back to the porch. "Yep, they're at the desk."

I locked eyes with Nate, feeling heat flood my cheeks. So now we had a dinner date? Surely the day could only get better from here.

8

DINNER PLANS

Nate

Watching Elle's face flush was an ego boost, I couldn't deny. This girl had occupied any spare place in my mind for the past month. Her curves, freckles scattered like a constellation, they hypnotized me.

However, my attraction to Elle was more than that. It was how she interacted with everyone in the library. Her smiles as she watched the kids that came in for story time. How she twirled her hair when lost in thought. The ways her eyes lit up when she talked about writing.

Over the past month, I'd found myself drawn to her when she was at the library, asking questions and getting to know her. More than anything I wanted to take her on a date, and this dinner set up by Gabby and Ava seemed like a great idea. I wanted to high-five both of them and say thanks for being Team Nate.

"So, dinner?" *Please let her say yes.* I held my breath, sending up silent prayers.

Slowly, she nodded.

I worked to school my expression. My mom's constant

reminders to check in for consent, always, made me ask again.

"Yes, you're good with having dinner with me?" I prayed for another nod.

Elle took a deep breath. "Yes." She closed her eyes as she nodded. "Yes, dinner sounds good." Long exhale. "God, I'm sorry. My mind is going in a million different directions." She looked so uncertain, and I couldn't stand it.

I took a step forward. Then another. I reached the spot where she leaned against the railing on the porch and stood in front of her, not touching, but close enough that I could smell her perfume. It smelled like salt air combined with the woods and hit me in the gut as uniquely Elle. I wanted to lean forward, burry my nose in the nape of her neck, and wrap her in my arms. She had to be getting cold. Controlling myself, I gently put my hand under her chin, tilting it up until her eyes met mine.

"Elle?"

"Yeah?"

I lost myself in her eyes. They were a caramel color with what appeared to be a freckle in one iris. God, they were beautiful.

"Sweetheart, there is nothing wrong with you."

Elle's eyes closed, then she looked back at me, not moving from our position. "Thanks for saying that, Nate. It's been a day." Her eyes fluttered shut as her tongue poked out and slid over her lips.

Damn. I knew she wasn't doing that to be provocative, but I certainly felt it as my jeans began to get a bit snug.

As she titled her head, I considered that I'd do anything to be able to read her mind right now. The right corner of her lip slid under her teeth, and I prayed for willpower in my pants. Jesus, what this girl could do to me without realizing it.

"So you really are good with going to dinner with me?"

Laughter burst out, unbidden. "Did you not hear my comment earlier? I was down with the plan on that text message. And I am absolutely thrilled with the idea of dinner. But how about you? Those two inside seemed to have masterminded a date for us. Are you good with that?"

Elle seemed to stand up a little taller, though I still towered over her. "Yep, I'm good. Where do you want to eat?"

I gestured for her to go in front of me as we headed back into the library. "How about my place?"

Elle glanced back at me and paused. "Your place."

"You bet." I gestured for her to continue, and we moved past the circulation desk, rounding the corner, and headed to the table where Elle's laptop and bag still resided. I noted Gabby and Ava were perched on chairs there, watching our approach with some amusement. All they needed was some popcorn.

"Proud of yourself?" I whispered to Gabby as Elle tossed the strap of her bag across her body, sliding the laptop inside.

Gabby watched Elle, then looked back to me. "You guys getting dinner together?"

I nodded.

Gabby's grin was wide as she replied, "Then yes, I'm pretty proud of myself."

"Damn straight." Ava inserted herself into the conversation.

"Ava," Elle sighed.

I had a strong feeling that might be a common response to her sister. Ava seemed to be a force of nature.

"Where are you two headed for dinner?" Ava asked.

"My place," I replied.

Ava leaned to the side and high-fived Gabby.

I choked back a laugh as Elle appeared to be mortified. "Do you actually want us to go over any book list, or was that all a ruse?"

"Hell no, we're putting you to work." Gabby slid a document across the table. "That's a copy, so feel free to make notes on it and bring it to work tomorrow. We can finalize the list then. And Nate..."

I looked at Gabby. Her voice was filled with laughter. "Yes?"

"I'll be sure to let Grace know she won that contest we'd been talking about."

I growled.

Gabby rolled her eyes, then looked over at Elle. "Elle, you're in luck. Nate here is an excellent cook, so don't let him try to go the lazy route and order pizza or anything."

Elle glanced my way. "You cook?"

I slid a hand over my stomach as it let out a growl and watched Elle's eyes track my movements as her gaze heated up. That was it. I needed to get her out of there and away from the prying eyes of my friend and her sister.

"You bet I do. Let's go."

9

———————

WELCOME HOME

Elle

Breathing in a deep cleansing breath, I took in Nate's place. He lived about three blocks from the library, away from the downtown, in a small cottage. The brick walkway leading up to his house had a gentle curve. The snow had mainly melted off during the day, but there were still traces here and there in his yard. Three windows faced the street and lights shone from his front room, making the entire place glow with warmth and a feeling of welcoming.

"Did you come home earlier?" I asked as we came up the last step.

"No, why do you ask?" Nate pushed the door open and gestured for me to go ahead of him.

"The lights are on," I murmured as we stepped into a room that immediately felt like home.

The entire space was wide open, with hardwood floors, and the walls were clad in large white planks running horizontally. There was a worn leather sofa by the front windows as well as an armchair angled to the side that made me want to curl up with a book. Bookshelves wrapped the

53

lower half of the room, and what appeared to be barn beams on the ceiling gave some separation between the living room and the kitchen area. A large island divided the two, giving a defined cooking area behind it with windows into the backyard.

I scanned the room, noticing there were books strewn in several spots, as if one could sit down and grab whatever was nearest, finding something to read.

"Timers."

"Hmm?" I looked back to Nate, feeling like I was being pulled out of a dream. What the hell was wrong with me?

"The lights are on timers." He placed his hand on my lower back, gently steering me into the room so he could close the door. "That was the hardest part of living on my own." He dropped his coat and bag on a bench, then kicked off his shoes. "Beer?" he asked, moving toward the kitchen.

"Please." I dropped my stuff as well before heading toward the island. "And what does that mean, the hardest part of living on your own?"

With his head inside the fridge, Nate continued. "It's nothing, just a memory of home." Pulling two cans out, he held one up. "IPA work for you?"

I noted the label from the brewery in town. Nodding, I wondered if he was going to elaborate. "Continue." I grabbed the beer and watched him, in a bit of awe that I was standing in Nate's kitchen. This had been a day of surprises —both good and bad.

Nate leaned against the counter, looking at the beer in his hands, seeming to be lost in thought. Shaking his head slightly, he looked my way. "It's nothing, really. At least nothing bad. My parents are pretty fucking awesome, and I had a great childhood. But you know how sometimes you don't know what you have until it's gone?"

I nodded.

Nate paused, took a drink, then continued. "When I got my own place after college, I realized that all my life, at least through my teen years, when I'd get home after dark, my mom would make sure the lights were on when I was coming home. Whether she was in the back of the house making dinner or already in bed, the lights were there to welcome me."

I felt my chest fill up with the warmth in his voice when talking about his mom. Damn, that was attractive. "And you didn't like coming home to a dark house, so you got timers for your lights?"

Nate looked up with a shy grin. Wowza. A strong desire overtook me to slide my arms around his waist and lean in. I held back, but barely. Seemed that my confidence was coming back.

"Sounds lame, right?"

I thought briefly that he couldn't be more wrong. Hell, a guy that loved his family and the feeling of home so much that he worked to achieve it on his own? Yeah, I could get behind that.

"Not lame, it sounds like love." I continued quietly, "I'm glad you had that. Where are your parents now?"

"I grew up in a town about fifteen miles from here, and my parents still live in my childhood home, but this was my grandparents' place. I inherited it when they passed." He glanced around in what looked like wonder.

"Happy memories?"

Nate nodded slowly. "Hell, yes. Lots of great memories. My grandparents were a trip. My grandma loved to tell dirty jokes. My grandpa was happy just watching her. They were pretty awesome."

"Sounds like it."

"Yeah." Nate cleared his throat. "They both passed last year..." He trailed off, but then his voice returned. "But hell, they were in their eighties, had long, full lives. I try to remember that, not that I don't wish like hell I could have one last dinner with them here."

I looked around his home. While certainly on the small side, the space was used exceptionally well. I could easily imagine a small family growing up there. "These were your mom's parents or your dad's?"

Nate stood from the counter, placing his beer on the island before turning to the cabinets and rummaging through them. "Mom's. She was an only child. So am I." He smoothed his hand over the worn butcher-block counters. "I spent a lot of time here growing up. When my parents let me know that this was mine, that I could live here, well, I couldn't turn that down. Getting this place helped me make some important decisions about the direction of my life." His voice lowered. "It makes them feel closer in some way, you know?"

I nodded. Glimpsing the stack of books next to the couch, I smiled. "Clearly you like books." I jerked my head toward the living room. "Is that something you've always loved?"

Nate's laughter was easy with the lighter topic. "Heck yeah," he said. "I don't remember a lot about reading in elementary school, but in fourth grade, I read *Hatchet* by Gary Paulsen and I was hooked. I'd convince my grandpa to take me to the woods and talk to him for hours about how I'd survive if I crash-landed in the wilderness."

His gaze landed on the trees just outside the kitchen windows. Damn. I'd thought he was attractive when I watched him in the library over the past month. My feelings had grown when we talked and I got to know him. But this?

Relaxed in his home, sharing memories that left him vulnerable? This was kryptonite to any remaining willpower I had. I just hoped he was being honest at the library earlier, that whatever was between us wasn't one-sided. I didn't know if I could handle it otherwise.

10

MAKE A MOVE

Nate

I wasn't sure what it was about Elle that had me spilling all my feelings within minutes of having her inside my home. I'd much rather return to the conversation we were having on the porch of the library, if only to get to be that close to her again. Or talk to her about whatever shitstorm that was happening at her work. Yet I didn't want to rush her or make her feel like the only reason I asked her back here was because of any physical attraction. There was that, certainly, but this seemed like it was possibly so much more.

Elle moved to the living room and was scanning the stacks of books I had on the floor and on the shelves. Turning, she asked, "So do you have a favorite type of book?"

I organized the ingredients for dinner, pulling items from the fridge and cabinets so I'd be ready to go. "Not sure I have a favorite type. I'll read anything. If I'm just reading for me, I'd say I probably gravitate toward books that have a bit of suspense."

Elle returned her head to the side tilt she had going on

while she scanned the spines of the books. Murmuring, she said, "Like Patterson."

"Yeah, I think I have a few James Pattersons in there, but I also have authors like Mary Higgins Clark that I used to read with my grandma."

Elle's cheeks flushed. "Sorry, not trying to stereotype you as a reader..." Her voice trailed off.

Pulling out a skillet, I tried to think of a way to put Elle at ease. She was a study in contrasts—confident at times, unsure at others. "Elle, it's just books. I mean, we could pull up my list of books on my eReader and discuss my favorite romance authors. Books are books. You aren't going to offend me in this conversation. Promise. Now how do you feel about chicken in a creamy chive sauce?"

Elle stood across the island. I couldn't help but note that her mouth was open, as if in surprise. It was freaking adorable.

"Thoughts on chicken?" I prodded.

Elle's eyes refocused, then narrowed. "Umm, where do I start?"

"Chicken."

She smirked. "Chicken is good. Now let's get back to this professed love of romance books."

Quirking an eyebrow at her, I turned to place the skillet on the stovetop. Dropping a bit of butter into it, I began to dredge the chicken in flour as the pan heated up. "Professed love? Nope, I said it outright. Romance books are some of my favorite things to read."

I moved from preparing the chicken to check on the skillet and see if it was warm enough. Seeing it still needed more heat, I turned to see why Elle had gone radio silent. She stood there, brows drawn, watching. Damn, she was gorgeous. What was even more attractive was that she seemed to have no idea how she affected me.

Looking at Elle, I was hit with the idea of what could be. For a month we'd danced around this attraction. I thought it was just me, but lately I'd felt more certain that I wasn't alone in that dance. And now I knew I wasn't. Even with that knowledge, I had a strong desire to take this slow. Elle wasn't someone to rush. I wanted to savor this, every step of this beginning.

But man alive, it was hard not to.

"Elle, you look like you have something to say." I reached over to grab some chicken and placed it in the skillet, hearing the sizzle that told me I'd waited just long enough to get the perfect brown on each side, but it wasn't so hot that everything would immediately be scorched. Looking over my shoulder, I prodded. "Come on, out with it."

Elle shook her head slowly, then paused before moving forward to claim a stool at the island. Sliding onto it, she said, "I just hadn't pegged you as a romance reader."

I assembled the white wine, cream, and cut lemon to the side of the stove. Grabbing some fresh chives, I began to chop. "So are you someone who looks down on romance books as smut? I wouldn't have pegged you for that, Elle."

Elle began to stumble over her words, she was trying to reply so fast. "That's not, I mean, I wasn't trying to say, that."

I was torn between wanting to laugh and the need to put her out of her misery. I decided to put her out of her misery. "Elle, I'm giving you shit."

"Oh." She focused on the counter, then took a deep breath and looked me in the eye. "I'm sorry. Sometimes I revert to a nervous high school kid and stumble over my words."

I took a breath and debated my next move. I flipped the chicken over to brown on the other side, then moved from the stovetop to the island. Taking a breath, I slid my hand across to capture Elle's. "Let me try that again, Elle, because I know for damn sure that my intention is not to make you nervous."

"Okay."

I almost forgot what I was going to say as I looked into her warm brown eyes. "So what I should have said, Elle, was that I love romance books. How do you feel about them?" I traced my thumb back and forth across her hand.

Not moving her gaze from mine, she bit her lower lip, then whispered, "I love them."

"What do you love about them?"

"The HEA, I mean, the happily ever afters."

"I work at a library, Elle. I know all about HEAs. Hell, Gabby and I run the romance book club filled with half the retired ladies in town. Once in a while we might get a guy to attend. So I get that I'm not the typical market for a romance book. Doesn't mean I can't appreciate one."

Elle began to move her thumb over my hand, grazing my palm. Damn if that didn't make me want to vault the island to get to her. Just as I began to convince myself to round the island and kiss her senseless, I smelled the chicken.

"Crap." Dropping her hand, I spun around and grabbed the spatula. I scooped up each piece and moved it to a plate I had to the side, checking the bottom to see if I'd burned it. Hmm, a little browner that I would've liked, but not bad.

"So what do you like about romance books?" Elle asked as she watched from her perch.

I poured the wine in the skillet, allowing it to come to a boil before it reduced. Keeping an eye on it, I turned slightly to Elle. "What's not to like? As you mentioned, I'm a sucker for a HEA. But also, I think some of the best books out there right now are romance books. I mean, you can read smart characters like anything from Penny Reid, crazy and hilarious stories from Kristen Ashley, gorgeous historical from Courtney Milan, and that's just a start. And of course there's the queen, Nora Roberts, that Lou in town always jokes is my long-lost relative. I think that's just because Lou would lose her shit if she could meet Queen Nora."

"Damn." Elle let out in a breath.

"What?" I poured cream into the skillet with the reduced wine and swirled it together before adding some lemon juice and chives. Then I placed the chicken back in the skillet and lowered the heat. My rice cooker was already on the counter, ready for dinner tonight. I rinsed the rice and got it started before turning back to Elle.

She'd been watching me but now stood with an uncertain look. I could sense the hesitancy in the way she leaned forward, then paused. As much as it killed me, I stood still. Elle had to be in charge here. She needed to decide to make a move.

Come on, Elle. You've got this.

11

CARPE DIEM

Elle

Get your ass in gear, Elle. Claim that man.

Hmm, interesting. Apparently, Ava's voice was now in my head. Voice of reason? More like the voice of the devil. Still, I was trying to locate my lost confidence and move myself around the island.

I took a step, then another, and before I knew it, I was toe-to-toe with Nate.

"Hey." I gathered all my courage, but my gaze locked on his socks. Specifically, I noted the script on them. *Carpe the fuck out of that diem.*

Well said, socks. Well said.

"Hey." He stepped in front of me and watched my gaze.

I nodded, trying to confirm I was exactly where I wanted to be.

Nate placed a finger under my chin and lifted it up so he could meet my gaze. "Glad you decided to move over here."

I slid my toes across his foot. "Apparently I'm working on seizing the day."

Nate slid his hands to my hips, tugging me closer to him. "Are you now?"

Come on. You've got this. "Yes, I am." Tilting my head to the side I nodded at one of his hands. "Looks like you are too."

"Just trying to follow your lead, Elle. I want you to be in the driver seat here."

I felt a tug of indecision as my stomach rolled with nervousness.

"Talk to me, Elle. What's going on in that beautiful brain of yours?"

For the past month I'd fantasied about a moment like this. I mean, the instant attraction when I saw Nate had quickly morphed into a *what if* scenario. But I liked Nate, I mean really *liked* him. While Ava was happy to date casually, I preferred relationships. But I hadn't had one for ages. And for whatever reason, Nate seemed too good to be true. I was tongue-tied around him, especially when we first met. Nerves that I hadn't felt for years flooded back. I had no idea what to do with this.

"I was just thinking about something else I like about romance books." I gathered all my courage and stared into his eyes. They looked like melted chocolate right now and were locked on me.

"What's that?" he asked as his hands caressed my sides.

I felt my face flush even as I knew I was going to say it. I thought about my grandma, as bold as they come, telling me that I'd regret only the chances I didn't take. Time to take one. Past time, actually.

"Sex scenes." I bit the corner of my lip and watched for his reaction. I wasn't disappointed.

Nate groaned. "Shit, Elle, do you know what you do to me?"

"What?"

He pulled my hips flush with his, and I could feel him, rock hard, against me. Damn.

One of Nate's hands moved to lightly touch my hair, playing with the ends as he seemed to work to control his breath. "Elle, would you be okay with me kissing you?"

My heart beat louder than a bass drum. "I'd be pissed if you didn't."

"I'm so glad to hear that."

I held my breath for a moment as Nate smoothed a thumb over my eyebrow before letting his hand drop down to tilt my chin in his direction.

"Elle, breathe."

As my breath whooshed out, he dipped down and his lips met mine. Holy hell. At first, they were soft, gentle. His teeth captured my bottom lip as they sucked it into his mouth, then let go. Then his tongue traced the seam of my lips before I parted them, letting him in.

The kiss began to build as my hands roamed from his back to his front. I tugged his shirt out so I could slide my hands up his stomach and to his chest. I considered throwing a leg around his hip and pulling him closer but thought that might be a bit much. Nate moved his lips down my neck, sucking in a spot gently, right at the nape. Then, just as I began to pant, he pulled away.

"What?" My head was spinning. Every hot scene I'd read in a Kate Canterbary novel flashed through my mind. I wanted to try them all.

Right. Now.

Nate leaned down and kissed the tip of my nose. Keeping his hands on my hips, he nodded at the island behind me. "Want to sit here as I finish this up?"

"Um, sure?" I started to put my hands back to help

myself up, but Nate put me up there before I could even get started. Well, that was hella hot, but what in the world? We were done?

Just ask, I told myself. "What was that?" I patted myself on the back.

Nate was stirring the cream sauce on the stove, flipping the chicken over that was sitting in it. "That was fucking amazing, that's what that was." He placed a lid on the skillet, then turned his focus back to me.

"I agree. So why in the name of all that is holy are we stopping?"

Nate gave me a look that made me want to whip off my top, lay back on the island, and let him do anything his heart desired.

Slow your roll, Elle.

He stepped over to meet my legs, moved them apart so he could stand right between them, and lightly grazed my lips with his.

"Elle, I'm not in a hurry...," he started.

"What if I am?" I got out like the hussy I was beginning to think I was.

He chuckled but then put a finger on my lips. "I like you, Elle. A lot, a whole lot."

I pulled his finger off my lips so I could respond. "I like you too." Then I placed his finger back.

Nate stood there for a moment, just staring at me. I could tell he was trying to figure out how to phrase something, so I waited.

Clearing his throat, he began. "Elle, I don't want a night. I don't want you just to jump me—"

My face flushed, I could tell.

Nate kissed my nose, then continued. "I mean, I'm all for that, but I want to start slow. I want to savor every experience with you. I want to make out on my couch to the point that I'm going crazy, but we still wait."

"You mean like waiting for marriage?" I strangled out. Then I looked around for a hole I could disappear in, crashing my forehead to his chest.

Nate's rumble of laughter reverberated through his body. "What I'm saying is I don't want to rush. You're important to me. In one month of quiet conversations at the library, I have gotten to know you. I know I would like to explore more with you." He ducked his head so we were looking at each other. "Do you understand?"

"Are you asking me to go steady?" My voice cracked as I immediately wanted to slap my forehead. Who the hell says *go steady*? I did, apparently, that's who.

Nate's eyes sparkled. "If we were in middle school, I could pass you a note that asked you to check yes or no about going out with me." He kissed my brow, then leaned back to watch. "What do you think?"

I felt some wetness in my eyes. Yes, I wanted all he was offering, and so much more. "I think I want that too."

My phone took that opportunity to vibrate across the counter from us. I glanced back and Nate said, "Check it. I need to stir this sauce one last time."

Tugging it toward me, I saw Ava's name on the screen. Of course. Opening the text, I saw several messages I hadn't heard come in.

Ava: *I'm feeling bad that I pushed you to leave with Nate. I mean, what if he's an axe murderer?*

Ava: *I mean, hottest axe murderer ever, right? But I'd still feel bad.*

Ava: *Elle, hello? I'm going to need a proof of life before I can go about my night.*

Ava: *You're just fucking with me now, aren't you?*

Ava: *Seriously, do I need to get Gabby and storm the castle?*

I started laughing as I read the texts. Nate cocked an eyebrow, so I handed the phone over. Scanning the texts, his smile grew before he handed it back.

"What are you going to say?" he asked, leaning back on the counter behind him.

I paused, looking at my phone, and then at Nate. Fingers flying, I sent a text, then held my phone out once more.

Nate moved back to his spot between my legs and glanced down.

Me: *No storming the castle. Following earlier directions and plan on jumping his bones. Love you.*

"I approve," Nate said, sliding the phone onto the island. Immediately it began to vibrate.

"I need to turn on do not disturb," I murmured.

"Let her message," he growled. "The dinner has about twenty more minutes, and I have plans."

I marveled at the feelings of completeness that washed over me. "I thought you wanted to wait. Care to share?"

"Waiting doesn't take everything off the table, my beautiful Elle," Nate murmured, his lips following my throat down and kissing the crook of my neck. "I plan on getting to know you a bit at a time."

Letting my head drop back, I felt arousal wash over. "Sounds good."

My phone vibrated again, and I glanced down, only to look up to Nate with a panicked feeling in my chest. "Oh shit," I whispered.

12

BROKEN PIPES

Nate

My gut clenched as I took in Elle's expression. What had been a gorgeous face that was relaxed and more than a bit turned on was now drawn, and she had an adorable crease between her brows. "What?"

She glanced from her phone to me. "It's Ivy. There's a pipe leaking from my apartment down to the new yoga studio below."

"Oh no. Did your apartment flood?"

"No, it looks like they caught it quickly." She scrolled on her phone as new texts came in, then continued. "Kristine noticed it in the studio and got Ivy, who brought in a plumber. But they're closing the studio for a few days, and Ivy asked if I can go stay with Ava while they work on my place." She looked down at her phone, thumbs flying as her brows drew together.

I moved to the stove, turning down the heat to low. We might need some extra time. "So you think you'll stay with Ava?"

Elle bit her lower lip as she read what looked like

another text. "Well, she has a one bedroom. I think I could sleep on her couch. Or, hell, worst case I could share her bed. We did when we were kids."

"Or you could just stay here." The words were out before I even realized it.

Elle's head shot up, her eyes locked on mine, as my heart kicked into a new gear.

"What?"

Was I committing to this? Yes. Yes I was. Why the hell not?

I held my hands up. "I'm not trying to rush you. Remember our earlier conversation. I'm just saying I have three bedrooms in this place and only use one. It seems silly for you to be without a space of your own for several days when you could easily stay with me. Seriously, it's no hardship."

The corner of her mouth kicked up. "No hardship, hmm? What if you aren't able to keep that whole *let's take things slow* life motto with me living here?" She raised her eyebrows at me from across the counter. "Will that be a hardship for you?"

Hell with this. I turned off the burner because I couldn't be trusted not to ruin the whole damn dish right then. And Elle being sassy and confident made me want to devour her, though I beat that back. She watched as I moved back to her, then gently took her phone and laid it on the counter.

"I have a proposition, Ms. Robinson."

She arched one eyebrow. "Yes, Mr. Roberts?"

I slid my hands onto her hips, running them over her curves. What this woman did to me was criminal. "It's like this, Ms. Robinson. I've really liked getting to know you over the past month." I pressed my lips to her forehead. She tilted her neck to the side, and I followed her silent direction, letting my lips trail down her neck.

"Six weeks, Nate."

I nodded. "Yes, six weeks." I pressed a kiss to her collarbone. "So I think we look at this text from Ivy not like your day went downhill from whatever that shit show is you have brewing at work, but as a gift for us to get to know each other even better."

Elle ran her hands up my back. "Are you saying we will get to know each other *biblically?*"

I took a step back and observed her wide smile as I cheered inwardly as she felt more and more comfortable being herself. *More of that, Elle, more of that.*

"Oh no, Ms. Robinson. I think we absolutely need to still take this slow. The biblical knowledge will come." I leaned in to kiss her forehead, then stepped back. "But tonight, after the day you've had, I'm offering up a kick-ass dinner, beverage of choice, and bingeing some Netflix series on the couch. That is, unless you'd rather read." I gestured to the living room. "As you can see, I have plenty of material."

Elle's eyes went a bit watery. "Am I dreaming? Surely you are mythical, right?"

I paused, not sure how to respond, but felt it needed to be with some care. Why me wanting to take care of her would provoke tears was something I needed to figure out. "Not mythical, no. And not all my intentions are innocent, Elle."

"Do tell," she murmured as she blinked back the waterworks and looked to gain some steel in her spine on the spot.

"I mean, I do want to help you out. You've had a hell of a day. And it seems ridiculous to crash at Ava's when I have a perfectly good spare room or two here."

"And you want me in the spare room?" She arched a glorious brow in my direction with a look of disbelief.

"Well, want and need are two different concepts, as my mom liked to tell me growing up. But for tonight, I need you there so I can stick with the plan."

"And that plan is..."

Why did it feel like this was such an important conversation? Like you-better-not-fuck-this-up type of conversation? "I want to get to know you better. I want to give you a safe place to land after a rough day. And"—I leaned over, placing my hand on her waist before tugging her to me—"I want to absolutely get to know you in the bedroom and out, but not today. Today has been a lot."

Elle stepped into my arms, wrapping hers around me and resting her head on my chest. "Nate?"

"Mm-hmm?"

"Thanks. It has been a day."

I moved to pressed a kiss to the top of her head, then lower. I was dead serious about taking this slow, *ish*, but her neck was sending out a call that I couldn't ignore. "So you'll stay?"

A sigh vibrated through her body as she tilted her head to the side, clearly asking for more.

"I'll stay. How can I repay you?" She raised an eyebrow at me.

My dick perked up, and I said some silent words to tell him that it was not the time. "How about you help me with that listing for my place in Chicago?"

She slapped a hand to her forehead. "Shit, sorry. I got sidetracked earlier. Yes, we can absolutely get that done. And we still have to look over that book list for Ava and Gabby."

"Yep, we'll get that done. And you'll give my whole *take it slow* idea a try?" My lips trailed up and down her, apparently not understanding what message I was trying to get across.

"Tonight." She let out a small gasp and moved in even closer. "Tonight we can take it slow, as long as that's what this apparently is. After that, we'll see."

I nipped her collarbone. "I like this take-what-I-want version of you, Elle."

"Not sure where she came from," she murmured. "Maybe that's what happens when your life gets shot to shit."

I moved back, thinking of her texts about work this afternoon and now her apartment. "How can I help? Do you want to go to your place now and grab some stuff?"

She rose up onto her tiptoes and pressed a kiss to my cheek. "You're supersweet, Nate." She stepped away and picked up her phone. "Address?"

I rattled off my address to her without question.

Elle shot off a text. "There," she said as she placed the phone back down. "I've asked Ava to swing by and grab some stuff for me and told her I was staying with you. If we're lucky, she'll actually pack items I need and not just what she thinks you'd like."

I gave some thought to what Ava thought I might like. That could be interesting.

Giving Elle a glance, I stepped back to the stove and switched the burner back on. "So Ava will bring your stuff here?"

She glanced back at her phone, another text coming in. "Yep. In about an hour."

I flipped a few pieces of chicken over, checking to be sure they were done. "Perfect. As soon as this heats back up, we're in business and can eat before she comes." I grabbed a towel to wipe down the counter.

Elle came to join me at the stove. "That looks amazing."

I glanced at her over my shoulder and smiled. "It is and it's done. You ready to be dazzled?"

"Already am."

13

PIPE DREAMS

Elle

The scent of bacon could wake me from a coma. Of this I was certain. My eyes opened, and it took me a minute to get my bearings. A glance around the room served to remind me that I was waking up in Nate Roberts's guest room.

Let's pause on that and rewind. Nate. Roberts's. Guest. Room.

My day yesterday was certainly one for the record books.

Nate was true to his word last night. We had a delicious dinner. Gabby hadn't lied, the man could cook. Ava had texted that she left a bag of clothes for me on the porch. Apparently she thought she might interrupt us, so she didn't want to ring the bell. That wasn't embarrassing at all. Nate found that I was between books, so he'd proceeded to book talk several for me until I picked up a romance by Naima Simone. Then we'd sat in opposite corners of his couch while we read for hours.

I was ready to profess my love. I mean, was there a more

perfect night out there? No. The answer was no, there wasn't.

I glanced again in my bag at what Ava had packed. I supposed I should be grateful that she'd included actual clothes. I'd figured she'd only pack lingerie, but she hadn't. That being said, my favorite uniform for working from home of yoga pants and a baggy T-shirt was conspicuously absent. Ava had what I thought of as my city clothes in the bag. When I'd first moved to Chicago and began working for Smithfield, my paycheck had helped my self-confidence jump up a few notches. Or more than a few. I found out that I liked purchasing clothes, looking nice. Once I got over the whole let-me-wear-baggy-shirts phase to disguise my breasts, I began to own my curves and stopped trying to hide them.

Interestingly, I hadn't been doing that down here. Looking at the clothes in the bag, Ava was telling me not to become a complete slob or try to hide away. I grabbed a pair of slim jeans, a chambray shirt, and a soft cream sweater. Fine, Ava. Message received.

A shower later and I felt close to human. I layered on a few necklaces to go with my outfit and gave myself a cursory glance. Not bad. My stomach growled, and I followed my nose to see what Nate had whipped up, hoping he had enough for two.

Coming around the corner to the kitchen, I paused at the view of Nate's back. He stood in front of his sink, washing some dishes. Bacon, eggs, and toast were piled on plates behind him on the island, but he stood washing a skillet as he hummed along to music that was quietly flowing from a speaker on the counter. At first I couldn't take my gaze from him. His hair was clearly still tousled from bed, with the front standing up straight. My throat went dry as I contemplated what it would be like to roll over in the morning and see Nate Roberts on the pillow next to me. Shaking my head, my focus came back to the kitchen. My gaze dropped over the threadbare T-shirt that was taut over his shoulders but loose at his waist to what appeared to be a pair of worn jeans. Then I listened a bit closer to the music flowing from the speaker.

I cleared my throat. "Is that"—I paused—"Bruce Springsteen?"

Nate stopped singing and looked over his shoulder at me. He took in my dressier-than-normal outfit, and his gaze heated. Meeting my eyes, he nodded to the speaker. "It is. Surprised?"

"It's just a little older... You're a fan?"

He turned back to the sink, rinsing off the skillet and then placing it on a towel. He turned to me as he dried his hands before tossing the towel over his shoulder. "My parents love him. He's the background music of my child-hood. This album, *Western Stars*, is a newer favorite."

I paused, listening. My parents were fans of his as well, but I didn't recognize this album. I refocused when I real-ized that Nate was walking toward me. As he came to a stop in front of me, I glanced down at his bare feet.

I was standing in front of him, and we both had bare feet.

Why were his so sexy?

And why did this feel like a level of intimacy that would have been far from anything I could have dreamed of had you asked me yesterday morning?

I looked past him, out the window to a wonderworld of white. "It snowed." I stated the obvious.

"Mmm-hmm." Nate stepped forward and dropped a kiss on my forehead. Hmm, so we were picking up from yesterday, not ignoring the fact that we'd become friends who kissed hello. I was on board with that plan.

"You look sexy as hell, Robinson."

Yum. I wanted to climb him like a tree. Slow, Elle. He wanted to go slow.

Why was that again?

Trying to move my brain off the track that screamed it wanted to go to the bedroom, I glanced at the plates of food. "You made breakfast?"

"Yup. Figured we'd eat while I went over the info for my apartment listing, if that works for you." He placed a hand on my lower back and steered me toward the island. I noted that my laptop was also there. I let him pull out a stool, and I hopped up, grabbing a napkin from the counter and placing it over my lap.

I forked up a bite of eggs, and flavor burst forth as soon as it hit my tongue. Holy Jesus, this put all scrambled eggs I'd ever had to shame. I looked to Nate with what could only be an incredulous look. "What on earth did you do to make these eggs so unbelievably yummy?"

"Low and slow," Nate said, wiping off the corner of his mouth. "My grandmother said it was the secret to amazing eggs, and she was right, as always. She said Europeans took their time with eggs and it showed. Americans cook them too fast and at too high of a heat."

Of course we did. I gestured at my laptop. "Okay, what do I need to know about your place?"

Nate finished chewing some bacon before talking. "I emailed you photos of my place, an overall list of what features you might want to note, and a few comps."

"Cool," I said as I opened my computer to pull up the information. I quickly found the info Nate sent and opened the documents.

"What were you writing at the library yesterday?"

I glanced from my screen to him with a quirked brow. "What?"

He gave me a measured look. "What were you writing?"

I thought back to yesterday at the library. "Umm, some work stuff?"

Nate nudged me with a handful of toast. "Was that it?" His voice was skeptical.

"Why do you ask?" My heart was hammering as it did anytime I thought of my book.

Nate put down the bacon in his hand and wiped his fingers on the napkin. He swiveled to put a knee on either side of me.

With a glance in his direction, I put my napkin on the counter and turned to face him. Nerves swarmed my belly. He looked serious, and I couldn't figure out where this was going. How did we go from a discussion about his condo to whatever this was?

"Sweetheart, did you know that when you are working on writing fiction, your entire appearance changes from when you're working on work writing?" His hand came up and tucked a lock of my hair behind my ear.

"What? How so?" My cheeks heated up because I had been working on what I called my pipe-dream project yesterday.

Nate's thumb skated up my jaw to my forehead and rubbed between my brows. "When you're working on work-work, your brows crease here and you look frustrated." He leaned forward, pressing a kiss to the spot. Pulling back, his brown eyes found mine and his voice softened. "And when you're working on your dream project, your entire face softens and you fight a smile as you type."

I didn't fight the smile that popped up at his comment. "That's nice," I murmured.

"It is, Elle. So why aren't you trying to work on that dream project more?" He sat back, watching me.

I looked away, my gut alight with nerves. "Dreams don't pay the bills, Nate. My job pays well, and I can't just give it up."

"Babe, look at me." His voice was serious but kind. Springsteen sang on about stones, and I wanted to wrap myself around Nate and skip this conversation. "Remember who you're talking to. You've told me about the agent who you met. The one who wants to represent you, to shop your book around. Why aren't you doing that?"

Yep. My cheeks were on fire. Why had I told Nate about this dream I was still holding on to? I'd met the agent at the convention hall last summer near one of the publishers' booths. We'd seen each other at these things over the past four years, and I still didn't know why I'd shared my idea with her that day, but she'd encouraged me to take the young adult historical fiction novel that was dancing around in my head and put pen to paper, or fingers to keyboard, and get back to her.

I wanted to, I really did. Since I was a kid, my dream had been to be a novelist. But now? Now that I could actually try? What if I failed? My job might be boring, but it was reliable.

I loved my story. But sharing it with the world seemed like taking a piece of my soul and letting others hold it up to the light to judge and deem worthy. I didn't know if I could risk it.

I looked to Nate, my eyes watery. This story, this dream —I wasn't sure if I could examine it right now, even with Nate.

"Can we talk about something else?"

Nate watched me, then leaned forward and placed a chaste kiss on my lips. "Okay, babe. I want to come back to that another time, but we can let it drop for now."

"Maybe we can talk about your listing?"

He considered me for a moment. "What do you have on your schedule today?"

My brain scrolled through my day. Sue had told me to step back a bit and lie low as they figured out what was going on at Smithfield. I was ahead on all my assignments. I needed to do a bit of work for the spring catalog, but that could wait.

"I'm open, why?"

Nate picked up my hand, entwining my fingers with his. "Today's my day off."

"And?"

His eyes twinkled. "How do you feel about Christmas tree shopping?"

14

TIMBER

Nate

I pulled into the parking lot with Elle by my side. A glanced in her direction confirmed that she was still lost in thought. She looked different today, good, but different. However, she also had a lot going on in that beautiful brain of hers, which was why I suggested a trip to get a Christmas tree. She deserved some time to step away from the stress surrounding her—with work, with her apartment. I hoped last night did that somewhat and, fingers crossed, today would some more.

I know I'd told her we needed to move slow, which I was now second-guessing like crazy, but so far, I was determined to stick with it. I wanted to give her a soft spot to land, a safe place. I hoped that once she felt like she was on firm ground, we could build something from there because, make no mistake, I wasn't looking for someone to share a night with. After knowing Elle for only six weeks, I knew I wanted more with her. A whole lot more.

"We're here," I said. I slid out of the 4Runner and

moved around to her side to find her shivering as she shut the door.

"Brr," she said, tugging her stocking hat over her ears as she turned to face me. She looked over my shoulder. "This is busier than I thought it would be."

I glanced around. Even for a Tuesday morning, there were folks out here. "It looks like there are a few field trips out here right now." I gestured at some of the small buses that local preschools used. "You met Max Harp at the brewery the other night, right?"

"Emma's fiancé?"

I nodded. "I've gotten to know Max and Sully, Emma's brother, a bit when they've swung by the library to see her. And of course at the brewery. Anyway, Max works out here at Highland Woods. He's been working to make it a spot for kids more than it's been in the past. They've always sold Christmas trees, but this year..." I gestured at the snowy wonderland in front of us. "He made it a bit more."

"I don't even know where to look first," Emma said. "The red barn is just too perfect. And is that"—she squinted toward the barn—"a hot chocolate stand?"

I smiled. "Yep. I think Max is using Emma and Sully's grandmother's famous recipe."

"Nate, is that..." Her voice trailed off with excitement as she looked toward the trees where, sure enough, a horse-drawn sleigh was coming out.

"A horse-drawn sleigh? Of course. What is a tree farm without one?" I laughed. "Max decided to offer sleigh rides when talking to one of the preschool teachers in town. She lamented there isn't enough to do with her kids during the winter outdoors. He's had them out here for short nature hikes, so this was his next plan."

"Can we," she started to ask before her voice faltered.

I turned, placing my hand under her chin and lifting it up to meet my gaze. "Ask for what you want, Elle. Always."

I watched the flush creep across her cheeks even as her lips tipped up in a grin. "Okay. Nate, do you want to go on a sleigh ride?"

"With you? Hell yes. How about we get some hot chocolate and take a ride?" I steered us toward the barn and sent up a note of thanks to the Fates. A busted pipe in a wall that led to Elle becoming my roommate and a sleigh ride together? Life was pretty sweet.

Twenty minutes later our sleigh set out on the trails. Blake, a local college student who worked part-time for the park, told us we'd come out at the perfect time. A half an hour earlier we'd be waiting in line for a ride with a crowd of three- and four-year-olds. As much as I enjoyed story time at the library and my regulars, I was glad they were already on to a nature hike and we'd missed the exuberant crowd. Here was hoping they'd be on the bus and headed to town for a nap by the time we got back.

Blake seemed inclined to let us stay cocooned in our bubble together in the back of the sleigh while he steered us around the park. I pulled the blanket up on Elle's lap and looked to see that her attention was on the scenery sliding by.

"Warm enough?"

Her eyes came to mine, and she smiled. "Yes, thanks." She took a sip of her hot chocolate. "This is delicious."

"It's the same mix we use in our coffee at the library."

"Ahh, that's why it's familiar." She took another sip, then looked back to the woods. "Thanks, Nate. This is amazing."

I wrapped my free arm around her, thrilled when she snuggled into me. "Anytime, Elle."

She gave me a side look. "So you're not regretting offering up your guest room yet?"

"Hell no." I took another drink and debated how to wade into this conversation. My dad would say straight on is the only way to go, so that's what I did. "So yesterday was a bit rough for you."

She let out a shaky laugh. "Yep, you could say that."

"Any word on the job or the busted-pipe front?"

She slid her phone out like it was going to give her an update. "Not much, I guess. I had texts from my boss saying they'll talk to me in a few days after they finish their internal audit. Ivy said they'd gotten to the pipes before much damage was done. Nothing was ruined for me or the yoga studio beyond some walls, so that's the best scenario that could have happened there. They're waiting on some plumbing parts, and I should be able to go back at the end of the week."

She glanced to me. "Can you handle a roommate for three more days?"

I bit back the retort that she could stay indefinitely. My house already felt more like a home with her there than it had since I'd moved back. She felt like my missing piece. My heart told me to dive in. My mind said to give her a solid foundation, especially when her world was in a bit of disarray. Instead, I replied, "Of course."

I stacked our now-empty cups together and put them in the corner of the bench seat. We sat in silence as the sleigh bumped over the ground. Blake was murmuring to the horses as he steered us toward the mansion in the park. Home of the original owner of the property in the early 1900s, it was now a conference center and housed the offices for the park and a café.

We turned the corner, and there it was up on the hill, a pond below, all blanketed in the morning snowfall.

"God, that's gorgeous," Elle breathed out.

I looked at her, her nose rosy from the cold, eyes alight with emotion. It sure was. She was. And I couldn't hold back. "I need to kiss you, Elle."

Her face tipped up to meet mine. "No one is holding you back, Nate."

Scooting closer to her on the bench, I framed her face with my hands and pressed a kiss to her lips. They opened on a breath, and my tongue slid in, finding hers, and beginning that dance. I felt, as I had the first time I kissed Elle yesterday, that I was where I was supposed to be.

That with her, I'd found home.

Her head tilted to the side a touch, allowing me to deepen the kiss. Her arms slid around my waist, and I pulled her as close as we could be, sitting side by side.

I'd kissed many women in my twenty-seven years. Kissing Elle was different. In every possible way.

We pulled back at the same time, and I searched her face, trying to decode where she was at in this freefall of a relationship we found ourselves in.

"I love kissing you," she said, breathless.

I laughed. I loved that she wasn't holding back. "I love kissing you too."

"Just saying, I'm still here," Blake called from his spot, humor lacing his words.

"Thanks, Blake," I shook my head with a grin at Elle.

"We're turning here," Blake said as the horses made a wide arch. "Back to the shed in about ten."

Elle and I settled back into the seat, blanket up, my arm around her. As we returned to that comfortable feeling between us, I returned to our conversation from the morning. Really, it was a continuation of the conversation we'd been having in pieces since she shared her dream with me so many weeks ago.

"How goes your story?" I asked, pressing a kiss to her temple in the hopes that it would keep her relaxed. Instead, I felt her body tighten.

"Easy, Elle. I'm not here to make you do anything you don't want to do. I just want to understand."

I felt her take a breath, working to let go. "It's not easy, Nate. I don't think you understand how scary it is."

I worked to hold back a laugh because I knew she wouldn't take it the way it was intended. "Elle, you know I moved down here only five months ago, right?"

Her uncertainty of where I was going with this was clear from her voice. "Yes?"

"I left the fifth largest library system in the country to move to one of the smallest ones. That meant a pay cut, a loss of stability, a loss of access, you name it." My fingers ran over her shoulder, trying to send comfort through her jacket, to help her relax. "I'd been on the staff for years, but I gave it up to come here."

She let her head drop to my chest. "I hadn't thought of that. Why did you make that choice?"

I found myself twirling her hair around my finger. "I wasn't happy. In Chicago, I felt like one of many. I was lost in the crowd. I stopped and thought hard about where I'd felt at peace in my life, and my heart called me home. Then my grandparents passed and left me their place, and the call grew stronger. And when there was an opening at the Ryan Library, I knew where I belonged. It was worth the risk, worth the lifestyle change."

"And you're happy with your choice?" Her voice had a dreamlike quality. Like she was processing what I said but not completely here. I hoped that meant she was thinking about her own situation.

"My grandma always told me that if I had a choice, to choose what made me happy, even when it scared me. So I chose my happiness. I don't think you can go wrong when you do that." I let my head drop back against the sleigh, looking up into the winter sky, trees lining the trail on either side of us as we neared the barn.

"So, simple as that? Choose happiness?" Elle whispered beside me.

"Choose to follow your heart, Elle," I said back, rolling my head to the side to watch her as she looked down the trail. "See where that leads you. Then you can't go wrong." Her eyes met mine, and I prayed she could absorb the belief I had in her. "Believe in yourself, choose your dreams, choose you. You're worth it."

15

FULL STEAM AHEAD

Elle

The bed in Nate's guest bedroom was hidden under a pile of clothing. Pretty sure I had emptied the bag of everything Ava had packed, to no avail. I'd been debating what I was wearing out tonight for the past twenty minutes. If I kept it up much longer, I'd be late.

Quite frankly, considering I hadn't seen Ava since Monday and it was Thursday night, she'd been patient. At least for Ava. I'd sat back from my computer a little over an hour ago and realized my phone was lit up with text messages she'd been sending while I was engrossed with catalog copy.

Ava: *Did the hot librarian tie you up and decide to hold you hostage?*

Ava: *I mean, not to make light of the whole idea of hostages because some weirdos in this world make that a reality I don't want to contemplate or I'll never use a rest area again.*

Ava: *And let's be real, my bladder is too tiny to follow through.*

Ava: *But seriously, sis, where the hell are you?*

Ava: *If I don't hear from you in the next hour, I'm pulling in the big guns.*

Ava: *And by guns, I mean Mom. You know I think some folks have seriously misinterpreted the second amendment in this country.*

Ava: *But I digress.*

I laughed out loud reading through her messages. My big sister, ladies and gentleman. She was a unique human being.

Her last messages were from thirty minutes ago. Hopefully she hadn't messaged our mom. She and Dad were traveling right now, but I knew she'd gladly team up with Ava to check in on me. Nope, that was something to avoid, though I did love my mom to pieces.

Me: *Chill, Ava. I was working. What's up?*

Ava: *Hal-le-freaking-lujah. I was wondering if I should round up some police officers and check on you. Though, to be fair, not a hardship. Have you met Ben Jones yet? Not hard on the eyes.*

Ava: *That being said, girls' night. No getting out of it. Ivy, Gabby, and Emma are in. Ivy's talking to Nic and Kate. We're meeting at Homestead in an hour.*

Ava: *I realize that's earlyish, but I'm not on Christmas break yet, so we're just doing dinner and a drink or two. Can we pry you away from the hunky roommate for that long?*

Me: *I'm in.*

I looked at Ava's texts for a long moment, soaking them in. Just over two months ago, Ava had suggested I move to this town, assuring me that I'd find what was missing in my life.

It wasn't Nate, as nice as whatever this was going on between us. Ava had meant I'd find community, and she was right, I had. Nic and Kate were two of my neighbors above the bookstore. We hadn't had one of our rotating dinners this week because of the busted pipe, so I was excited to see them.

But these friendships, this feeling of belonging, wasn't the only benefit of moving here. I was also finding myself.

I wasn't sure how to describe it or even if I could. But it was like each day put a piece of the puzzle that was me together.

I think if the shit had gone down at work when I was still in Chicago, I would have stressed. What if I got taken down by those on social media because of my professional relationship with this man? I knew I had done nothing wrong, but according to Sue, it was looking pretty damning for him. He was going to need to examine his biases and do some work to understand his privilege and how he'd used it to the detriment of others. As Ava had taught me over the years, it's not enough to say you're not racist, but you need to work to be an anti-racist. Anti-racism is about action, realizing you might fall short at times, but working to eliminate racism.

My colleague wasn't there. According to Sue, he was still in the world where white privilege didn't exist, and he didn't see what he'd done to cause any issues.

Smithfield was committed to not dropping him as an author and professional development educator, but he was going to be expected to do some learning. They were working on some company policy, and I'd be helping them draft statements in a week or so.

Yeah, a few months ago, this would have consumed me. I would have worried about some Twitter user lumping me with my colleague and painting me with the broad brush for his actions. Now, I was not owning his mistakes. More than that, thanks to talking to Nate, I was examining my dreams again. Could I take the leap?

But that wasn't for tonight. Tonight was for girls, for fun. Nate had told me he was working, then would be home. I was all in for meeting Ava.

However, I was going to be late if I didn't figure out some clothes, and quick. I sent off a text to Ava.

Me: *How dressy?*

Within a minute, Ava's reply lit up my phone.

Ava: *This is Highland. You can wear anything you want. I'll be there in a few.*

Well, that didn't help. I glanced out a window and noted the snow still blanketing the ground. Warm, I needed to dress somewhat warm.

Hell with it. I was overthinking everything. What did I feel like wearing? I grabbed a light gray cable knit, skinny—yet comfy—jeans, and a scarf. I pulled it all on and turned to look in the mirror over the dresser in Nate's guest room. Not bad. Scarf draped around my neck, I turned to grab the down vest as my phone vibrated with another text.

Patience, Ava, patience, I thought as I glanced to my phone.

The smile at seeing Nate's name, not Ava's, was instantaneous.

Nate: *Hey, beautiful. What are your dinner plans?*

Me: *Funny you should ask; my sister has coerced me into a girls' night at Homestead.*

Nate:...

Worry ate at my stomach as I waited for his reply. We were roommates, but also more, though I wasn't sure how to define that more yet. Should I have run my plans by Nate first before committing to Ava? Damn.

Nate: *Perfect. Hope you won't think I'm stalking you, but Max invited me to hang at the Homestead with him and Sully tonight after I get off work. Is that okay or do you want space?*

Damn, this man was perfect. Right? Right.

Me: *Stalk much? Kidding, kidding. I think the Homestead is big enough for both of us. I'll try to resist you.*

Nate: *Don't try too hard.*

Whoosh. My belly felt like it was a shaken bottle of soda, ready to explode. Another vibration from my phone had me hoping for another message from Nate.

Ava: *I'm outside. You ready?*

I glanced to the mirror and nodded to myself. I was absolutely ready. And maybe some girl conversation tonight could help me with how to convince one Nate Roberts that this take-things-slow plan had been a good plan with good intentions, but it was time to throw it out the window.

Quite frankly, I was ready to move full steam ahead and was ready for him to hope aboard. Literally.

16

CUT TO THE CHASE

Nate

It was an exercise in frustration to watch Elle across the brewery. She and her group had been at some of the high-tops in the bar for the past hour. I'd seen them and felt the magnetic pull that I always did when she was around. I wanted to let her know that I'd posted her listing for my condo this morning and already had several inquiries. A friend up there was showing it a few times tonight and tomorrow as a favor. Elle clearly knew her shit, and I was grateful. So grateful that I'd been working on a surprise for her. I hoped it would express my gratitude and let her know that she had someone in her corner.

So why was I in the tank room across the brewery from her, getting glimpses from the windows that looked out into the main room? One, I wanted to give her space. I knew from what she'd said that one of the reasons she moved to Highland was that she felt isolated in Chicago. Clearly that wasn't something she was struggling with in Highland. It looked like her group ranged from her sister to her neighbors to some of my colleagues. It was weird. I almost felt proud of her in some way. At any rate, I wanted her to have her night, even though a large part of me wanted to claim her as mine and let no one near her. Was the caveman tendency a latent one?

"How's the roommate situation working out?"

I was pulled out of my thoughts by Max Harp, who sat next to me at the high-top by the windows.

What to say?

"Well, it's going." That was a start, right?

Max chuckled, placing a beer before me. "Barn Owl stout good?"

I nodded, taking a drink. "Thanks."

Max settled onto his stool, and his partner in crime, Cole Sullivan, or Sully, came up to join us.

Max gave him a look. "Surprised Maggie let you out tonight."

Sully laughed. "More like pushed me out. She said she was watching something on Netflix, going to bed early, and didn't want me hovering."

I shook my head with a smile. Maggie was Sully's wife and Emma's best friend. By my best estimate, she might have three weeks left in her pregnancy, maybe two. She taught at the middle school and often came by the library to visit with Emma while lamenting the fact that she could no longer see her feet.

Sully turned his focus on me. "She did send me out of the house with the strict order to find out what was going on with you and Elle. Sorry, man. She's in the uncomfortable part of pregnancy here. I can't go home empty-handed."

Our server, Lauren, blessedly interrupted us to drop off the food. I ignored Sully and Max for a moment to eat a wing. Dropping the bones into a spare bowl, I glanced across the table to see them both watching, waiting.

Jesus. "Sorry to disappoint. Not sure if I have much to report."

Max snorted. "Not what I heard from Blake."

"The kid you have working for you?" Sully asked, smiling as he looked from Max to me. Keeping his gaze on my face, he asked, "What does our Blake have to report?"

"Well, apparently Mr. Roberts here took Ms. Robinson on a quaint little sleigh ride on Tuesday morning," Max said, warming up.

Sully's smile widened as he rubbed his hands together. "That's the shit romance books get written about. Nicely done, Nate."

"And"—Max paused for effect—"Blake might have mentioned that their lips happened to fall on each other at one point."

Sully nodded like he was thinking it all through, rubbing his chin. "Makes sense, makes sense. If you wandered into a damn Hallmark movie, you'd need to continue on brand, right?"

I shook my head at them as my gaze was drawn to the windows again to check on Elle. Her head was thrown back as she laughed while her sister walked around the table, high-fiving their crew. I looked back at the two gossips I was sharing a meal with.

"Fine, so maybe we do have a little to report. But we're taking things slow," I cautioned.

"Man, she is *living* with you," Sully said, eyebrow raised.

"In the spare room," I pointed out.

Max about lost his beer. "I'm sorry," he said. "What?"

I felt my face flush. I didn't have brothers. I had close friends, but we were more likely to talk about the White

Sox or the latest concert we'd been to, not any relationship we might be in. Was this supposed to be the norm?

"I didn't want to rush anything," I said, my voice trailing off as I felt all the indecision I had inside well up.

Sully gave Max a look, then glanced my way. "Maggie said you two have been circling each other for six weeks."

"Well..." Truth, but how did I explain that this meant something to me and I didn't want to fuck it up?

Max's grin widened. "Sul, I think our boy here has it bad."

Sully nodded, he stood up and came to my side, clasping my shoulder while nodding seriously. "Nate, we've been down this road before you..."

"Sorry I'm late," Jake Spencer, the other brewery owner, came in the door to the taproom.

"Just in time," Sully said. "You can join us in educating young Nate here."

"Um, I think I'm only four or five years younger than you all," I grumbled.

"A lifetime," Sully said with a smirk. "As I was saying, you can learn from your elders here, young friend. We've all"—he gestured to Max, then Jake, who was filling a beer at the tap on the wall, then to himself—"found our lifelong partners in the past year. We know what it means to find that woman who changes everything. And we know how scary that can be."

"I mean, to be honest, we all know that Maggie can be terrifying," Max said with a wink. "And though Ivy is sweet as hell, she self-identifies as a green witch, so I think I'm the one that got off easy here."

"Emma is hell on wheels when you piss her off," Sully said of his sister.

"Oh, don't I know that." Max grinned and raised his eyebrows.

"Fuck off," Sully growled at his friend.

"Drew should be here for this," Jake said, pulling up a seat by me.

"Where is Drew tonight?" I asked. I'd met Jake's brother at the Reds event here last week.

"Hanging out with Ivy's daughter, Addie so we can come here," Jake said. "Now, back to you. Someone fill me in. Why is Sully dispensing his questionable wisdom?"

"Well—" I began again.

"He has Elle in the guest bedroom and is taking things slow," Sully replied.

Jake raised his eyebrows and looked at me, then to the window where you could see Elle and company across the bar. He did a slow pan back to me as he cut to the chase. "Cut that shit out and make a move."

Max laughed and Sully toasted Jake.

I looked back to Elle. I mean, what had I been thinking? Maybe it was time to remove the training wheels off of this relationship. I thought we were finally up to speed.

Elle and I stepped out of the brewery into the winter evening. She tipped her head back to look up at the sky, so I paused beside her to do the same. We stood there for a moment as we looked up together.

Finally, I broke the silence. "Are we looking for something in particular?"

Elle stood there for a moment, then whispered, "No. It's just this place. I mean, it almost feels magical sometimes."

I thought about that. "You mean because of the quiet?" I looked over at her.

A smile spread across her face, lit by the light from the brewery. "The quiet, the clean smell of pine, the fact that people wave at me when they pass me on the street, *even if I don't know them.*"

I laughed. "Want to walk for a few minutes before heading back?"

"Sure," Elle said. "Do you care which way?"

"Nope."

She moved toward the downtown and the bookstore. I fell into step beside her, reaching out to intertwine my fingers with hers. She squeezed my hand, and I squeezed hers back.

"You have fun tonight?"

She let out a contented sigh. "Yes." She paused, then asked, "You know what I still can't get used to?"

"What's that?"

"When I walk into the brewery or the deli or the pizza place, everyone stops and looks to see whose coming in. Do you notice that?"

I thought about it for a minute. "Yeah, I guess I've gotten used to it."

"That doesn't happen in Chicago."

"Well, maybe in small neighborhood places. I think folks just assume there's a good chance they'll know the person that's coming in and want to say hi."

Elle laughed. "Or they're nosy."

"True."

Elle took in a deep breath filled with contentment. "Nate?"

"Yep."

"I smell snow."

We turned in to the downtown. The snow earlier this week still blanketed the grassy areas by the courthouse. The white lights strung around the square joined the old street-lamps to bathe the whole area in a warm glow.

Elle stopped, let go of my hand, and spun around with her arms out. Light flakes were falling as she laughed and threw her head back. She was gorgeous.

"I feel like I'm in a snow globe," she said.

I took a step toward her. Then another.

"Elle," I murmured.

She stopped spinning and looked at me. "Yes?"

"I feel like if I don't kiss you right now I'm going to combust."

Her smile was instant. "Well, we can't have that." She reached out, grabbed my jacket, and pulled me toward her.

My hands framed her face as I dropped my forehead to hers, breathing in her scent. She smelled of cinnamon and vanilla. She smelled like something I wanted to wrap around me and never let go. Her arms encircled me, pulling me close as my lips found hers.

With absolute certainty, I knew this was where I was meant to be.

17

UNDER THE CHRISTMAS TREE

Elle

Nate and I walked back to his place, touching constantly. Tonight was amazing. My belly ached from laughing so much. It had been exactly what I needed, almost. Every once in a while, I'd feel a prickling sensation and look up to see Nate watching me from the taproom, where he sat with the guys.

Ava had commented on it and laughed, saying we should just head home and dive into bed because we were going to burn the place down with the sparks flying between us. Maybe I should have felt like it was creepy to have his eyes on me so often, but it felt amazing to me. I felt wanted, desired, and God knows I wanted him.

But I stayed out with my friends, and we had a great time. Just when I got up to get my coat so Ava could drive me home, Nate had appeared at my side, asking if I wanted to walk with him. Ava had given me a knowing smirk and taken off. We'd headed outside, walked a bit, and then he kissed me.

He *kissed me.*

It wasn't like it was the first time we'd kissed, but part of me kept waiting for one of our kisses to feel just *okay*, like any other time I've been kissed. Instead, each kiss seemed to be better than the last. Nate made me feel special in a way I couldn't put my finger on. Tonight's kiss promised more.

As we walked home, I hoped that meant that he was done with this *let's go slow* nonsense. I mean, quite possibly that had been a good call on Monday night. Monday had been *a day*. Work, having to move out, having my sister push me into a date with Nate.

Well, that part had been good, great even. But it was a lot. By Monday night, my head had been spinning. The guy that I'd crushed on, slowly getting to know for over a month, the guy I'd shared my secret dreams with, had me staying at his house? I mean, come *on*. So while I had wanted to do anything but go slow, Nate likely made the right call.

Days later, however, I was feeling more secure. My place hadn't had any damage. Work was work, but there was a plan there that, in the end, would result in better education for us all. And I'd spent the past three days at Nate's house, getting to know him, being reaffirmed daily that the guy I'd been falling for all this time was even better than I'd thought.

Life was good.

A tug at my hand pulled me out of my thoughts.

"You good?" he asked, coming to a stop in front of me, running his hands up and down over my arms.

"Yeah," I whispered, losing myself a bit in his eyes. *Ask for what you want, Elle*, I chastised myself. Deep breaths. "Nate?"

He leaned in and kissed my forehead, then stepped back a bit to meet my eyes. "Yeah?"

"Do you think—I mean, don't you think..." I bit my lip, unsure.

Nate gently brushed a kiss across my lips. "What, babe?"

Go for it. I thought. "Don't you think we could be done going slow now? I mean—"

I didn't get the rest of the sentence out as Nate's mouth was immediately crushed against my own. His lips parted and I wasted no time, my tongue immediately sliding in and finding his. We kissed like we'd be interrupted at any minute and needed to devour each other before that happened. Though, to be fair, in this town someone could be along at any time, so maybe it was time to move this indoors.

I pulled back, chest heaving, and looked at Nate. His eyes were locked on mine.

His lips tipped up into a grin. "So you want to move things along, do you?"

I nodded, possibly vigorously. I mean, I wasn't hiding anything at this point.

He brushed my hair back and over my shoulder as his other arm slid around my waist. "How much did you have to drink tonight?"

Hold on. I needed to pick myself up off the sidewalk. I mean, seriously. *This man* was better with each conversation. "One beer, when I got there. At least three hours ago."

He nodded as if that made the decision for him, then leaned forward and pressed a kiss on my neck. Then another. And another. Goose bumps rose up everywhere as I contemplated what this could be like without pesky clothing in the way. As his mouth moved back up, it stopped by my ear and he whispered, "Let's go in."

My heart threatened to beat out of my chest as I

looked from him, then in the direction that he stepped, his arm keeping me next to him. I hadn't realized we'd stopped in front of his house; my focus had been clearly on getting Nate to eliminate the word *slow* from his vocabulary.

Moving up the walk, something seemed off. I looked at Nate's house, trying to piece it together, before stopping in my tracks.

Nate glanced over his shoulder. "What's wrong?"

My eyes tracked over his place, "Where are your welcome-home lights?"

Nate smiled and slipped his arm around my waist again. We moved up the final steps before he unlocked the door and stepped back for me to enter before him. "Why don't you see for yourself?"

I stepped through his front door and stopped. The living room was lit by the glow from the white lights on the Christmas tree in the corner. We'd brought it home on Tuesday, but Nate had said he usually left it up for a few days before decorating, which allowed the branches to relax a bit.

I'd loved the pine scent which permeated the entire house. My parents were big fans of artificial trees, not wanting to deal with sweeping up needles on the regular. But this tree, sitting in this room and reading next to it, I might become a convert for life.

"You put the lights on," I said, completely unnecessarily.

"Just the lights," Nate said, shutting the door and coming to stand behind me. He wrapped his arms around my waist and rested his chin on my head. "We can decorate it together, but I wanted you to come in and see it all lit up."

"When did you do this?" I said in a hushed voice. For

whatever reason, there was a magical feeling in the air and I didn't want to disturb it.

"After work before coming to the brewery."

I turned in his arms and looked up to find that he hadn't taken his eyes off me. "Nate?"

"Yeah?"

"Thoughts on skipping the bed for our first time and having sex under the tree?" The Ava voice in my head cheered out loud. Maybe Nate had been right to take this slow because I felt far more comfortable asking for what I wanted than I ever had before. I wasn't questioning it but following my gut.

Nate's smile widened as he leaned down and captured my mouth with his own. Stepping back, he looked me over. "Babe, that sounds like the best idea you've ever had."

He pressed a kiss to my lips and then stepped back and unzipped his jacket and pulled off his stocking hat, dropping them on the sofa. His brow arched in my direction, so I did the same. We kicked off our shoes and then stepped around the coffee table. Nate ran his hands over my sweater as I unwound my scarf and tossed it over his shoulder toward the couch.

His fingers were at my waist and hovered at the hem of my sweater. "May I?"

I nodded and then it was up and off, tossed somewhere onto the floor. He grabbed his own shirt, and it quickly followed.

I worked to school my breath. I wanted to go in so many different directions I wasn't sure where to begin. My mouth wanted to kiss Nate all over. I wanted to get my jeans off, and his, to get this party started. I wanted to pull him against me so we were skin to skin. I was paralyzed with indecision.

Nate helped out by unbuttoning his jeans and pushing them down in a rush, so that he stood before me in boxer briefs and nothing else.

Whoosh. My jeans fell right off. No, not really. I quickly shed them, but it sure felt like it. My mouth was dry, my happy place was, well, happy and not dry by any sense of the word. Damn.

Standing in front of Nate in just a bra and underwear, I marveled at how comfortable I felt. The me of the past, the self-conscious young girl I was even in college, would be thinking about my soft belly, larger thighs, more-than-a-handful breasts barely contained by my bra. But now... I watched Nate's eyes take me in and heat up, clearly wanting more. I felt good about who I was and, importantly, what we were about to do.

Nate grabbed a blanket from the armchair and spread it on the floor under the tree. He held out his hand to me, and we lowered to the blanket. I rolled to my side to face him, the glow from the tree all around us.

"You still with me, Elle?" he asked, his hand sliding up my arm as he moved closer.

"Absolutely," I whispered.

He slid one bra strap down and pressed a kiss to the swell of my breasts. His hand moved to my back, and he looked at me for affirmation. I nodded and my bra loosened. I shrugged it off, and it joined the rest of our clothes somewhere.

I started to push my underwear down, planning to do the same to Nate's, but he stopped me.

"Hold on, I just need to do this first," he said as his mouth worshipped my breasts. I mean, that's the only way to describe it. He moved to one side and kissed me all over until his mouth closed over my nipple and sucked on it.

Without any direction from me, my hips began to arch as my nipples both tightened in arousal. A tightening in my core begged for release. Foreplay was great, but I could get where I needed to go without it and right now. I was ready. Hell, I'd been ready for some time.

"Nate," I panted.

His mouth came up as his gaze shot to me, concern etching his features. "Do we need to slow down?"

"Hell no. We need to speed up. Maybe round two can be slower?" I grabbed my underwear and shoved them down until they reached my calves so I could kick them off.

"What?" Nate asked, his eyes now heated.

I reached over and put my hand on his cock. I lightly squeezed, which elicited a moan from him. "This. I need this in me. Five minutes ago wouldn't have been too soon."

A bark of laughter bubbled out of him. He shoved his underwear down before rolling over to grab what I could only assume would be a condom out of his wallet.

Rolling back to me, he pressed a kiss to my lips. "Elle, I love the way you think."

18

CIRCE, THE ENCHANTRESS

Nate

I sheathed myself in a condom before rejoining Elle. Part of me wanted to see if I was dreaming. She was a vision. Her body was gorgeous normally, but in the white lights glowing from the tree above? She was breathtaking. The tree branches made patterns on her skin that made me want to trace with my tongue. However, she said she wanted to move things along, and who was I to deny her?

As I moved to her side, I pressed a kiss to her lips because it was all I could do. "Elle, I love the way you think." I whispered. As I let my lips move to her jawline, I debated on positions. I mean, there wasn't one I didn't enjoy. However, normally when I had sex, I started with oral. I knew it was tricky for women to orgasm by penetration alone. And believe me, working with mostly women, I'd long ago adopted the mantra of women come first. But I trusted Elle to know what she needed, so there wasn't a chance in hell that I was going to deny her request.

Her mouth moved to my neck as she nipped it. My cock jumped. If I wanted this to happen, I better get moving. I was quickly coming to a place of no return. My dick was telling me we were short on time, and I needed to make this good for Elle before that happened.

I slid my hand to her ass to hold her to me and rolled to my back, pulling her on top of me. Her hair cascaded on either side of her face, enclosing us in this space together.

"Smooth move, Roberts," she said with a smile.

"Think so?" I said with a smirk. I pulled her head down to press a kiss to her lips. Letting go, I watched her face in the lights. "You still sure about this?"

She smiled as she ground herself against my shaft. My eyes closed, and I groaned as she giggled.

"Temptress" I growled.

Elle leaned down, letting her tongue trail down my neck to my collarbone. Moving back to my ear, she practically purred. "Ready?"

I looked at her. Mesmerized. Taking a breath, I answered, "More than."

She slid up, notching me at her entrance, then slid down as we both exhaled.

Holy shit.

Fully surrounded by Elle, I prayed to all that was holy that I could last long enough to make this good for her. Her hands moved to my chest as she sat up and began rocking. Lord help me, I could lie there watching her and be damn satisfied. She was Circe and I was under her spell, helpless to be anywhere but here. Luckily, that worked just fine for me.

I began to thrust up, angling myself to work to hit her g-spot. I reached a hand up to pinch one of her nipples.

Elle hummed each time I thrust, and one of her hands moved to her clit and her fingers began to circle as she grew louder.

"Damn, Elle, you are a vision." My voice was huskier than normal. The walls of her vagina were pulsing, and I worked to hold back just a little longer. Watching her take charge, get what she needed, was unbelievably sexy.

"Nate," she whispered, "are you close?"

"Fuck yes," I said, thrusting up again. "Go, babe."

She cried out, and I felt her clench around me. Pulsing once, twice, and then I was lost to it, the sensations shooting up my spine until I felt like I shattered.

Elle dropped to my chest, boneless, and I wrapped my arms around her. She turned her head to one side, resting her ear to my chest. We both panted, like we'd just run a race, and I trailed my hand up and down her spine, soaking her in.

As we came down, I pressed a kiss to the top of her head. "You okay?"

She laughed as she leaned up, propping an elbow on my chest so she could look me in the eye. "Okay doesn't cover what just happened, Nate."

I curled up to press a kiss to her lips. "I'm glad to hear that, Elle, because I'm beyond okay too."

Her eyes twinkled in the lights as she looked at me. "I believe I said something about round two taking more time than round one."

I fell back to the floor. "Are you trying to kill me, woman?"

She moved to hover over my face. "No complaints, sir. Just wondering if we can move to a bed before any further festivities. That is, unless you were wanting me to go to the guest room..."

I immediately rolled us to the side so I could slide out. Taking care of the condom, I then stood up and grabbed Elle's hand to pull her up.

"Like hell you're going to the guest room," I said. Tugging so she'd follow me down the hall with a quick pass by the trash can, I led her to my room and wondered how much sleep either of us really needed tonight anyway.

I woke up in the morning to an empty bed. Rolling to the side, I pressed my face into the other pillow. Elle's scent was there. I had no idea what the smell was, but it was all Elle and I wanted to wake up to it every day from here on out.

I turned to my side table to grab my phone and check the time. Today I worked at nine, and it looked like I still had over an hour until I needed to be there.

I had no idea what time Elle and I finally drifted off last night. Suffice to say, the second time—and third—had been much slower after we'd taken the edge off. I wouldn't allow myself the memories of going down on Elle or her doing the same for me or I'd be late for work for certain.

Stepping into my bathroom, I noticed she must have stopped in there before leaving. The hand towel was on the sink instead of the hook, and there were notes of her perfume too. I took care of business and hung the towel back up, wondering what her plans for the day were.

The scent of bacon hit me the moment I stepped into the hall. As I drew closer to the kitchen, I heard music playing. I reached the opening and saw Elle's back, swaying in front of the stove, as she sang at a whisper. Listening, I strained to figure out what she was singing. Elle did a lot of things well, but I don't think anyone would be inking recording contracts for her soon.

Finally, I recognized it. "Taylor Swift?" I asked, getting her attention.

She spun in my direction, a flush rushing to her face. "Jesus, Nate."

"Sorry." I raised my hands as I moved closer to her. "What song?"

"Um." She bit her lip as she glanced toward her phone. "'Coney Island' from the *Evermore* soundtrack."

I found myself in front of her, inhaling all that was Elle. I wrapped my arms around her and looked down. "Morning."

She grinned up at me, beaming. "Morning."

"So about last night...," I began.

She rolled her eyes. "Yes..."

"When can that happen again?"

"Now?"

I groaned. "I wish. Need to be at work in an hour."

She rose up on tiptoes to press a kiss to my mouth. "Well, then back up, bud. I need to finish breakfast."

I looked behind her to see bacon already sitting on a plate lined with paper towels, and it looked like she might be set up for—

"French toast good with you?"

My stomach spoke for me, growling loud enough for the neighbors next door to hear. "Hell yeah."

"I made some coffee too," she nodded to the counter.

I moved over, grabbing a mug from the cabinet above from rote memory. I placed it down and immediately knocked over another coffee mug that had appeared on my counter with spoons in it.

"Sorry!" Elle said, turning to pick up the scattered spoons.

"What in the hell was that?" I grumbled, not completely awake without the caffeine yet.

"I wanted to pay you back for everything you've done

for me. After we had the hot chocolate at the woods the other day and you mentioned it was what you had at the library, I asked Emma for the recipe." She gestured toward a jar now sitting on my previously sparsely adorned counter. "I put it here for you along with some spoons to mix it in."

Towels out of place, spoons where none had been before—this woman had been in my house for five days and was changing up my routines.

I was here for it.

Or I would be when I could wrap my brain around it. Which would require some coffee.

I pulled Elle against me. "Thanks for thinking of me, Elle. Means a lot."

She looked up at me, beaming once again.

Yeah, I could absolutely get used to this. She had enchanted me down to my very core.

19

─────────

DAYDREAMS

Elle

I stepped out of the shower, drying off and thinking about the day that stretched ahead of me. After breakfast Nate had shared he was heading to work, so I'd said I was going to take a shower and would likely be in later. Honestly, it was nice to have a moment or two to myself just to breathe.

Stepping into the guest bedroom, I rubbed the towel over my hair as I headed toward my phone. Ivy had said my place should be ready for me to head back in today. Was it ridiculous that I was sad about that?

Probably.

No, definitely.

Whatever. Nate needed to have his place back. I mean, he'd been kind and all to let me stay here, but I didn't want to overstay my welcome.

I looked at my phone and saw that there was a message, but my heart sped up when I saw that it was from Nate, not Ivy.

Nate: *Have a great day. Hope to see you at the library, but left you something in the third bedroom too.*

Curiously piqued, I turned and headed to the other room. Nate said he didn't use it, so I hadn't checked it out yet. The door had been closed, and I hadn't wanted him to think I was a snoop. I reached the door quickly and opened it, wondering what he could have possibly left me.

I stepped in and took in the space. The room was roughly the size of the guest room I'd been staying in. At first, I didn't see what he could be talking about. There were some shelves and a couch on one wall. Nate had mentioned it when we'd talked about his place, saying that it also folded out to be a bed when he needed two beds for guests, but that didn't happen often. Turning, I looked on the wall perpendicular to the sofa where there was a long desk.

I moved to it. The desk itself was nothing special, gorgeous dark wood, but it was simply a desk. It had a large work surface and a cushioned chair. What called to me, however, was what was on top. There was a long, narrow bulletin board leaning back against the wall. Pinned to the board were several images and words. Over the past six weeks in talking to Nate, I'd described the story taking up space in my head. And the images on this board? It was like they'd been plucked out of my mind. Somehow Nate had found images to match my inspiration: for the dark-haired Peter, the girl next door Thea, the Parisian catacombs in the '20s, some gorgeous old libraries, and more. He'd printed them out and pinned them to the board.

There were also quotes. Some were writing inspired like THE SCARIEST MOMENT IS ALWAYS JUST BEFORE YOU START or A WRITER, I THINK, IS SOMEONE WHO PAYS ATTENTION TO THE WORLD. There were also quotes, I believe, just for me. YOU ARE ENOUGH was at the top of the board.

And then I saw a quote that I told Nate I was printing on a T-shirt. TAKE CARE OF THE SHIT THAT'S WEIGHING YOU DOWN. My sister had sent it to me in a text the other day when I was lamenting the issues going on with work. Nate had typed it up and had a gorgeous mountain in the background.

On the desktop was a note from Nate.

E-

FYI, it took less than twelve hours to sell my condo once I put up your listing. There were three bids, and I got it sold above my asking price. You know your shit and are damn good at your job. But here's a place for you in case you also want to explore that dream of yours. Who's to say you can't do both? I believe in you. I think it's time to make that leap.

N-

"Whoa." Crushing his note to my chest, I plopped down in the comfortable swivel chair and sat back. My brain was running in so many different directions. One, Nate had set up a space for me in his house to pursue my dream. Maybe he wasn't as anxious for me to get out of his way as I thought. Two, the space he did set up? This was the shit you find in a romance book. Maybe that was the advantage to having a guy in your life who read them. It was crystal clear he'd been listening to me as we talked about my story. And three? I couldn't deny that having someone see me as a talented writer was an ego boost.

Could I do this?

I was beginning to think I could.

I dropped the note and picked up the phone. My stomach fluttered with nerves, but I channeled my inner confidence and typed out a quick message.

Me: *I found the office and note. You are unreal and beyond kind. But why would you set up this space when you know I can get back into my apartment soon? And by soon, I think it's ready today.*

The library must not be super busy because I immediately saw that he was typing a reply. The butterflies continued to ricochet around my belly as I waited for the text to come in. I wasn't sure what I was waiting for or what I was worried about.

My phone lit up, and I quickly looked down.

Nate: *Trying to give you a reason to stay, if I'm being honest. Or at least a reason to spend a lot of time with me.*

I really, *really*, wished Nate was there right then because what did I do with a text like that? So he wasn't tired of me being there? I mean, he'd given me no indication he was, but part of me had worried he'd offered to let me stay just to be nice, and then we'd escalated our relationship at warp speed. I felt lost and unsure as to what this was between us.

If I was being honest, I was terrified to hope for what I truly wanted.

Nate: *I'm serious, Elle. I wish I was there right now because I bet your beautiful brain is swirling.*

Me: *Not sure about that beautiful brain comment, but I'll admit that I'm a bit blown away.*

Nate: *Seriously, it's time to dream big, babe. Let's visualize. You're sitting at that desk in the spring. Your laptop is in front of you. What's on it?*

I spun to face the desk and closed my eyes. Tears welled up, which was just ridiculous, but Nate was being sweet. The least I could do was work through the visualization with him.

Before I could text, my phone rang. I looked down to see Nate calling. Small blessings, at least it wasn't Face-Time. Before I could click on it to answer, he hung up.

What the hell?

And a FaceTime call immediately came in from him because of course it did.

I wiped away the errant tears as quick as I could before clicking to answer. Nate was there, clearly in the back nook in the kitchen at the library.

"Impatient much?" I asked, trying to go for a light tone so he wouldn't see how rattled I was.

He laughed. "Sorry. I was taking a minute to get coffee here and wanted to have this conversation before I had to get back in there. Figured talking would be faster than typing."

But it requires far more vulnerability, I thought.

"I can tell you're at the desk." Nate's voice was gravelly. "Close your eyes, babe, and let's dive in. Can you see yourself working in this space?"

I nodded.

"I'm glad, Elle. Okay, if you're sitting there this spring, what smells are around?"

I kept my eyes closed and let my heart dream. "I think I'd smell a candle. I love to light them when I'm writing."

"Good. What do you hear?"

"Chickens."

Nate sputtered, and I opened my eyes to see his face. There was a look of surprise there. "Chickens?"

My face heated. I hadn't intended to say that. It just spilled out. "Um, well, in my dream writing world, when I've thought of writing a story, I have a small house where I write and I raise chickens. And am surrounded by houseplants."

A wide smile stretched across his face. "You never fail to surprise me, Robinson. And I'd like to note, you just answered my text. You said this is what you imagine when you're writing your story. So that's what is on your laptop, correct? Your story?"

I bit my lip, nervous but excited. "Yeah, I think it is. Your note made me think. There is no reason I can't do both right now, write for Smithfield *and* work on my dream story. There're plenty of hours in the day. I can get it written, then see if anyone thinks it's any good..." I trailed off.

Nate looked away from the phone and nodded to someone off-screen. Then he looked back to me. "Sorry, Elle, I have to go. But babe, there is no way it will be anything but good. You are a brilliant writer, and I can't wait to read this story."

The warm feeling in me intensified and made me want to lie down and cry. I didn't know what to do with it. Emotion felt like it was pouring off me. Instead, I just looked to the phone and said, "Nate, thanks for my writing desk."

"I believe in you, Elle. See you when I get home."

Oh boy. I think I was in over my head. This man made me want so much—for myself, and for our future.

20

UNFAMILIAR EMOTIONS

Nate

I stared at the computer screen in front of me and wondered at what age life presented all the answers to you. Apparently, it wasn't the ripe age of twenty-seven because I felt like I had far more questions in front of me than answers. The biggest one right now was how Elle and I had moved from friendship a week ago to far more now? More importantly, how on earth did I keep us on the trajectory we were currently on?

Damn. Ivy had been in an hour ago to drop off something for Gabby and told me that Elle's place was good to go. I wanted to beg her to tell Elle it wasn't done. I wanted to go vandalize the place, make it so she couldn't move back in just yet. None of it was rational—I did realize that, promise—but that's where I was. And I had no idea what to do with any of it.

Letting out a pitiful sign, I let my head drop to the desk, resisting the urge to beat it again and again. Jesus. What the hell was wrong with me?

"What's the matter, pumpkin? Rough day with the

toddlers during story time?" Gabby's amusement was clear in her voice, even with my head on the damn desk.

"Nothing," I muttered to the wooden surface in front of me.

"You think he's coming down with something?" Emma's voice actually had concern in it. At least she was kind.

"Coming down with a case of the feelings." Gabby's voice was laced with sarcasm. "Men never do know what to do with them."

"I mean, I can teach some relaxation breathing if need be," said a voice that I wasn't as familiar with.

I opened my eyes and saw Emma and Gabby. They were standing with Kate, one of the owners of the yoga studio next to the bookstore. Also known as one of Elle's neighbors. I sat up, hoping I didn't look quite as pathetic as I felt.

"Oh, um, hey all," I stammered, feeling my face heat up. Dammit. Five days ago I was self-assured. I had a decent flirt game going with a girl I liked. I'd been happy with where I was and the decisions I'd made. And now? What the hell had happened to me?

Gabby shook her head at me, her disappointment visible. She looked to Emma. "It's worse than we thought."

I looked at them in confusion. "What?"

Emma gave me a reassuring pat on the shoulder as she hopped up to sit on the circulation desk. "Kate told us that the studio and Elle's place were good to go."

"Yeah, Ivy said the same this morning." I wasn't following. How did this affect them?

"You poor clueless man." Gabby practically clucked at me. Yes, I said clucked.

"What the hell, Gabs?"

Gabby and Kate dragged two chairs over from the table

to join our little group at the circulation desk. Well, at least we were the only ones in the library for the moment.

"Nate," Gabby said with all seriousness.

"Gabby," I repeated back in the same tone.

"Sweetheart, you and I run the romance book club in this place. You know what to do with emotions. What in the world is your problem?"

I looked from my two coworkers to Kate, who I didn't know well but who seemed kind, back to Gabby and decided hell with it. I needed help.

"I don't want Elle to move out," I said. "I realize that's completely irrational. And also some patriarchal bullshit. I also know, before you say it, that I do not get to dictate Elle's choices. Hell, we only kissed for the first time five days ago. But, there it is." I sat back, arms crossed, and looked at Gabby.

"Let me get this straight. We owe this fabulous mood to the fact that you finally got the girl but are worried you're going to lose the girl, and you can't handle all the feelings coursing through you?" Gabby had an evil smirk on her face. Emma laughed and then quickly covered her mouth. Kate was kind enough to bite her lips, but it sure seemed like she might laugh.

"Knock it off, Gabs," I growled.

"I'm just saying for a man well-versed in the genre of romance, for a man who is typically in touch with his feelings, you sure aren't using what you've learned." She shook her head at me. "Now Nathaniel, I would assume you would know that five days is a bit quick to be roommates..."

"Um, no. From what you all have said, both Emma"—I gestured to Emma—"and Maggie were living with their respective guys within days." I grasped on to anything I could think of to rationalize my out-of-control feelings.

"Easy, speedy," Gabby said. Aslan, her cat, hopped up on her lap, ready to be showered with attention. Gabby ran her hand down Aslan's back as the cat arched up into her touch and loudly shared her gratitude. "You know damn well that Emma and Max as well as Maggie and Sully had known each other for years."

"All true," Emma said. "Sorry, Nate."

"Well, true." I conceded. "But I have known Elle for over a month," I pointed out. That was better. Right? Aslan gave me a look of what could only be viewed as pity. Great. Pity. From a cat.

"Nate." Kate quietly spoke up. "What are you really worried about? Because I've talked to Elle this week. I've only known her for a short time, but she was ridiculously happy. And considering she told us that she had work stuff and then the pipe at her apartment, I think that's saying something."

I closed my eyes and took a breath. Most of the people I'd worked with, whether in Chicago or here, had been women. I'd gotten used to talking about personal problems. That's just what they did. I was also good at listening and giving advice if, and only if, they were actually asking for it. And with these three, as much shit as Gabby liked to give me, I was going to ask. Because I wanted to make sure I hadn't screwed anything up here.

I took a breath, ready to lay myself out there. "It just seems like we're taking a step backward if she moves back to her apartment. So today, I made her a space in my guest room to be her office. And now," I looked over my shoulder at the monitor behind me.

Gabby, Emma, and Kate followed my gaze. Gabby spoke for the group. "Umm, are those plans for a chicken coop?"

I dropped my head to my hands. "Yes." Breath. "I talked to Elle after she found the space I made for an office, and she shared that part of her dream is raising chickens." I thought about our conversation. "And houseplants."

"Talk to me about this office space, Nate." Gabby sounded like she was trying not to coddle me and wasn't succeeding.

I continued looking at the floor. My Converse shoes were looking a bit worn. "Well, see..." I debated how to share what I had created for Elle without betraying her trust. "Elle's told me about this dream she has. It involves writing, so I created a nook in a guest room for her."

When Elle had shared her idea for her novel with me over the past few weeks, I'd immediately started pulling up images that sort of fit the characters and setting and printing them off for her. At first I was going to put them in a notebook for her to bring to the library. We'd had a young adult author visit our town this year as part of an author series that Emma had worked on with the school and Ivy's bookstore. They'd shared that it was helpful for them when visualizing their story, so I thought it might help Elle. However, I'd transferred the pictures to a bulletin board the other day after picking one up and putting it in the bedroom. I'd hoped to make a space that would give Elle the confidence to go after her dream. I'd lost track of time and hadn't realized she'd be moving out so soon.

"I made an inspiration board for her. Hoping it would be a nice spot for her to work and maybe reach for something she thinks is just beyond her grasp." I sighed, not sure where to go with this. "And then I talked to her, and she mentioned in her dream there were candles, houseplants, and chickens." But she had said she was leaning toward trying to write her story. So there was that, even if it wasn't from my place.

"Nate," Emma's voice was gentle. Her hand grasped my shoulder, and I looked up to meet her eyes. "What you did took a lot of thought. I'm sure Elle is grateful."

"She is," I thought back to our conversation. "I know it shouldn't matter that she's moving back to her place. I don't know how to explain it. Like I was happy that I moved back here, I knew I made the right decision, but when I met Elle? When I began spending time with her? When she moved in? It was like everything was as it was supposed to be. And now? I don't want to go back."

Emma's expression was kind. "Maybe you need to talk to Elle about this. And remember, just because she moves back to her place doesn't mean she can't stay at yours sometimes. Or you at her place? Think of it like you all went on a quick trip together. Now you're back home and continuing the relationship."

"Agreed. It was like a trip to cause you two to finally stop circling each other and get to the good stuff. And it appears to have worked. Now keep that boat afloat and enjoy the journey." Gabby raised her eyebrows at me in a suggestive way.

"Jesus, you're worse than some of the middle school kids that come in here, Gabs." I shook my head at her.

The vibration from my phone pulled my attention away from my group therapy session. I saw Elle's name on the lock screen and couldn't hold back the smile as I reached for it to see the full message.

Elle: *Ivy said I'm good to move back. I was wanting to cook you a thank-you dinner tonight. Is that cool? If so, my place or yours?*

With just those words, the clench of my gut relaxed for

the first time since I talked to Ivy. I probably was over-reacting.

Me: *That sounds great. How about we stay at my place for tonight? We could decorate the tree?*

Elle: *That's right. We didn't quite get to the decoration part of the evening last night...*

Gabby began to laugh and I looked up.

"What?"

Kate gave me a knowing smile. "Not sure what you're texting, Nate, but you should know that your smile is wide and your face is flushed."

Ignoring them, I shot off a final text.

Me: *We'll see if we get it decorated tonight. I'm fine with more distractions if you are.*

And to think, just a few weeks ago, going home was a lonely endeavor. Now I would be counting the minutes until the end of my shift.

21

CHICKEN COOPS AND HOUSEPLANTS

Elle

I danced around Nate's kitchen, Taylor Swift's voice pouring out of his Bluetooth speaker. I'd talked to Sue today, and everything at Smithfield was going better than expected. The author who had caused some hurt with his words had finally spoken up and owned his mistakes. Not sure who had convinced him to have a change of heart, but he'd vowed to spend some time learning from what he'd caused and was the first one to sign up for the anti-racism program that the company was putting together. While I wasn't thrilled with his original comments and his reaction in the immediate aftermath, Sue had reminded me that the goal we should be looking for was willingness to own our mistakes and learn and grow from them. She was right, and I could only hope he learned and grew from this because Lord knew there were others who needed to do the same.

After talking to Sue, I'd sat at the desk that Nate had set up for me, thinking that maybe I'd get a few more emails done or plan out what I needed to accomplish today.

Instead, after sitting and simply staring at the images he'd tacked to the board, my fingers had itched to type. I'd opened the document where I'd started my story and wrote. And wrote. And wrote.

Three thousand words and several hours later, I'd looked up. What the hell was that?

I was both terrified and elated.

I was going to do this. I was going to reach for my dream. My phone vibrated, pulling me out of my desire to lose the rest of my day to writing. Looking down, I smiled at Ava's name on the screen.

Ava: *Thanks for coming out last night. I love having you in town.*

Me: *You officially on winter break now?*

Ava: *You bet your ass I am. Tonight's plans include comfy pj's, comfort food, and bingeing something on Netflix. But then the next two weeks are mine. I cannot wait.*

Deep breaths. I needed to make this real and hold myself accountable.

Me: *Need to tell you something.*

Ava: *Ohh, intrigue. Spill.*

Me: *Nate has convinced me to try my hand at writing a book.*

Ava: *...*

I watched the dots. And watched the dots. And my anxiety threatened to spiral until I finally saw the text come through.

Ava: *It's official. I want to marry Nate and have his babies. Cancel, reverse that. I'll let you marry him and have his babies. You're finally trying to write your book?*

Me: *What do you mean by finally?*

Ava: *Elle, this is all you talked about as a little girl. I'm not an idiot. I didn't think that dream just disappeared once you graduated college. I figured you just wanted to get some writing experience under your belt. WOOO HOOO! I'm so proud of you.*

Me: *Don't get too excited. Who knows if anyone will want to read it.*

Ava: *Silly girl, no one can read it if it's only in your head. I'm ready to cheer you on. You will rock this.*

Me: *Thanks, Ava. Now I need to go. Making dinner for Nate.*

Ava: *We'll talk about this sweet and domestic scene later. What are you making?*

Me: *Chicken Divan.*

Ava: *Whoa. Pulling out the big guns. I'll let you get to it and tell Mom to start booking the church for next summer. Love you.*

I shook my head at her message. My grandmother had apparently made this dish for my dad the first three times in a row that he visited them. She had liked to joke that it was what got him to decide to stick around. What I knew for certain, however, was that my parents were perfect for each other. It wouldn't have mattered what my grandmother served.

That being said, this casserole was comfort food from growing up. And part of me wanted to give that to Nate tonight. I wanted him to come home, be able to smell this cooking in the oven, grab a beer together, and just be able to talk about our days.

I already had the chicken and broccoli cooked and in the casserole dish. I poured the sauce on top and sprinkled it with cheese. Sliding it in the oven, I moved to set the timer. Looking at my watch, I was excited to see that Nate should be back soon. Grabbing a sponge, I wiped down the counter and moved the rice cooker closer to the stove, flipping the switch to let it do its thing.

The door opened, and I turned to see Nate walk in, shedding his coat and hat to the hooks by the door. I drank in the view. He had on faded black jeans with a red-and-black flannel shirt, a white T-shirt under it. And my favorite part, he was wearing his black-rimmed glasses. He didn't always wear them, but when he did, yum.

Nate turned from hanging up his coat, and his eyes found mine. "Damn, Elle, have to say I like coming home to you." His stride was long as he moved across the room to come to a stop in front of me.

"You do?" My heart felt like it skipped a beat.

Nate looked almost embarrassed for a moment as he looked away, then met my gaze again. "I need to share something with you because it's important and because Gabby, Emma, or Kate might tell you if I don't. I had a bit of an emotional crisis at work today."

My stomach sank and worry kicked in. "What? What happened?"

Nate stepped closer, wrapping one hand around me to rest on my hip. His other hand came to my jaw as his thumb trailed up and down it. A flush spread across his face. I watched, trying to place what emotion it looked like he was struggling with, and then my worry dissipated when I realized it was embarrassment.

"Nate... Do I need to call Gabby?" I asked to get the ball rolling.

He shook his head and smiled at me. I noted the stubble

on his face. I didn't think he'd had time to shave this morning, and I had to say, I was a fan.

"Nah. I'm going to own this. I freaked because Ivy came in and said your place was ready."

I tilted my head as I looked up at him. "What? Why would that make you freak?"

He bit his lip. I reached up and gently tugged it down with a finger. Then I rose up on my tiptoes and pressed a kiss to the corner of his mouth. No idea why, I just felt like he needed it.

His expression softened, and he pressed a kiss to my temple. Gahhh.

"It's like I said in the text, Elle. I didn't want you to leave."

I pulled back in surprise. Here I was thinking I had possibly overstayed my welcome, that maybe he'd only offered to let me stay out of kindness. I mean, I knew he liked me, but liking someone and having them move in were two different things.

"Really?" I said with a small gasp of surprise. "I was worried I had interfered with all your routines."

"Oh, you absolutely did," Nate said. "After living alone for some time, it's weird for things to not be where I normally put them. But the thing is, Elle, I also liked it. I liked having you in my space. However, the girls pointed out today that you going back to your place doesn't mean we're moving backward."

"No, we're definitely not moving backward." I whispered, wrapping my arms around him. "I want to move forward with you, Nate."

He ran his hand through my hair, then dropped both hands to my hips. "Excellent, Elle, because I want to move forward with you too." He took a deep breath, then let it go and leaned down to brush a kiss over my lips. "After listening to you on the phone today, your dream of candles, chickens, and houseplants, I knew I wanted all that with you." He paused and took a breath, letting it out slowly. "Elle Robinson, I realized today that I love you. I want a future with you." His warm eyes met mine.

Whoosh. The air went right out of my lungs. How could one person be this lucky? I looked up at Nate, my vision getting a little blurry, as I whispered. "That's really good because I know I love you, Nate Roberts. I don't know when it happened, but looking at the bulletin board you made for me, I knew it for sure."

Nate looked at me as we stood there in his kitchen. I felt comfortable and completely at home.

"So we love each other," he said.

"Yep."

"And we'll live apart."

"Well, for a while," I conceded. "But you can stay at my place, and I could stay here. I want to write here for sure."

His smile grew. "You want to write."

I dropped my voice, still in awe. "I wrote today."

His arms enveloped me in a tight squeeze that felt—I'm not sure how to describe it—safe? Secure?

"You wrote today?"

I nodded. "Three thousand words."

He moved and his lips captured mine in a kiss that took my breath away. Pulling back, he leaned down so that his face was inches from mine. "I'm not sure what would work best for you in terms of support here. If you want me to read as you write and cheer you on, I'm here for it. If you want me to read at the end, I can do that. If you need me not to read it, well, that might kill me, but I can try."

I looked at him and debated the merits of each option.

Then I whispered, "I think it might be nice for you to read as I go. I can go grab my laptop."

Nate squeezed to hold me in place. "You can grab the laptop in just a second. Two things."

I waited.

"One, what the hell is that smell? My stomach is going to begin growling any second."

"Chicken Divan."

"Okay, no idea what that means, but I can't wait to find out. Two, we're going shopping tomorrow for houseplants. I want you to have whatever you need to make the office yours."

"No chicken coops?" I teased.

He raised his eyebrows at me. "Clearly you haven't checked your email."

I looked at him, then ducked out of his arms and took off to the office to grab my laptop. Bringing it back, I set it on the island and opened up my email. Sure enough, the top of my inbox had an email from Nate. Opening it, I saw a note that said "This work for you?" and a link that took me to the most ridiculously over-the-top chicken coop ever.

"Nate, what the hell is this?"

He rested his chin on my shoulder as he looked at my laptop screen. "Well, I figured we can plan for the chickens over the winter. Then we're ready to hit the ground running as soon as we're done with winter, and maybe by that time, you'll be moved in for good."

I closed my eyes just to soak it all in.

Turning my head to the right, his mouth was there. I pressed a kiss to his mouth before pulling back. "Sounds great." Looking back to my computer, I pulled up my story and slid the laptop to the side for him while I went to check on dinner.

Nate pulled out a stool and sat down to read as I grabbed a beer from the fridge and passed it to him. As I moved around the kitchen, finishing up dinner, I realized that in only five days my life had become everything I dreamed of and more. I was living my greatest fantasy.

EPILOGUE
FOUR MONTHS LATER

Nate

"Elle," I called, walking in the front door to our house as I wondered where she could be. I'd gotten a text from her twenty minutes ago that simply said she needed to talk when I got home. I'd racked my brain, wondering she had to tell me. Maybe one of the chickens had gotten out of the enclosure again? That had been an issue at first, but I thought we'd fixed it.

"Back here," she called from the direction of the bedrooms.

I kicked off my shoes and headed back there. Everywhere I looked, I saw evidence of Elle in our home. I'd moved in to this place less than a year ago. I'd worked to make it my own, but it had still felt like I was borrowing it from my grandparents at first. However, in the three months since Elle moved in, she'd helped it become ours. There were photos from my childhood and hers scattered on the walls. There were also pictures of us—with our friends and on our own. We were building something here, and I was grateful.

I glanced into our room, but she wasn't there, so I continued on to her office. She'd been writing here more than at the library lately. I hated not seeing her as much, but was grateful the space had worked for her. Sure enough, when I came around the door, she was sitting at her desk. Her hair was up in a messy bun, and she had on a thin, long-sleeved shirt that fell off one shoulder with a tank underneath. One leg was curled up under her, the other foot was on the chair, and she was leaning on her raised knee as she looked at something on the computer.

"What's up, babe?" I asked, moving across the room and pressing a kiss to her head.

She dropped her head back, clearly asking for a kiss and not just on her head. Glad to oblige, I dropped my mouth to hers. As her lips parted, I let my tongue find hers as the kiss went from a greeting to a promise of more in seconds. I ran my finger over the swells of her breasts that I could see down her loose top. Finally, I stepped back and worked to catch my breath.

"Elle," I said, somewhat breathlessly, "you said you wanted to talk."

Her eyes twinkled. "No, I said I wanted to show you something. Look." She gestured toward her laptop.

Her email account was opened. I looked at it and immediately realized it was an email from her agent, Shana. Scanning it, I stopped and looked to her with wide eyes, before looking back, wanting to make sure I got this right.

"Baby, does this say that Shana sold your book?"

She nodded.

"Oh my God, Elle!" I spun her chair around, and she shot out of it, jumping into my arms and wrapping her legs and arms around me like a baby koala bear.

"Baby, congratulations!" I kissed her.

She pulled back and then put her hands on either side of my face. Her eyes were dancing. "Nate, remember how I said you couldn't ask me any important questions while I worked on my book for the past few months because I needed to focus?"

Yep. Heart skipping a beat or two. I was sure it was fine. Because I knew exactly what she was talking about.

I nodded.

She bit her lower lip. "Well, just to say, thanks for giving me that time. And anytime in the future you want to ask any of those life-changing important questions, I can hear them now. No rush."

Holy shit. We were doing this.

"Okay, baby. I mean, this wasn't exactly how I envisioned this. But I'm not wasting a second. Though maybe I should kneel down."

Her limbs tightened as her grin widened. "No, just like this."

I leaned forward, pressing a kiss to her lips. Moving just a few inches back, I looked into her eyes. "Elle Robinson, on October 28 I walked out of the storeroom of the bookstore and saw my dream girl standing in front of me. Every day since then you've proven what my heart already knew. You're it for me. I am so damn proud of you for following your dreams, for all the hard work you've put in over these past few months, and I can think of nothing better than spending the rest of my life cheering you on as you go for the gold. Will you marry me?"

Tears were coursing down her face and, to be honest, mine.

She started to speak, though her voice was thick with emotion. "Nate Roberts, I love you. I've been falling in love with you more every day since we met, and I can't wait to see how much more I love you when we're eighty. Thanks for helping me believe in myself. Thanks for seeing me for who I am. Hell yes, I'll marry you."

Elle's mouth found mine, and I walked backward until my legs hit the couch. I lay back, letting her stretch out on top of me.

Elle pulled up to look at me. With a smirk, she said, "I can't wait to tell Ava that I've officially hooked my hot librarian."

I looked at her, and we both burst into laughter. Yep, she hooked me all right. And I wasn't letting go anytime soon.

Elle and Nate will forever have a special place in my heart. I started trying to write a romance story back in April of 2018. I had no idea what I was doing, but Max and Emma kept talking to me, so I wrote. When I was "done" with their story, I had zero knowledge about how to publish, so I started writing Sully and Maggie. This went on and I figured these stories might just be for me.

Fortunately, the universe had other ideas. I joined my local RWA, Heart and Scroll, and learned a ton. There I found a small press looking for stories centered around books for a short story anthology. I wrote up the first version of this, weighing in at a little under nine thousand words, and sent it off. My students knew, I'd written it during NaNoWriMo as they wrote too, and cheered me on. When it was accepted I felt like maybe these stories I had weren't just for me after all.

Follow your Dreams, originally titled *Love at the Library*, was published as part of the *Book It* anthology in November of 2020. I knew immediately that I wanted to tell more of Elle and Nate's story, so I decided they'd be the perfect end to my first four books in Highland Falls.

To all of you that have gone on this journey with me thus far, I cannot thank you enough. I love romance books. When I started writing, it was because I *needed* a different kind of romance. I needed a romance that was low-conflict because I was anxious enough, filled with good people who looked out for each other in a small town with characters that heated up the pages. I hope I've done just that.

My hope is to publish three more books in the next year. Fingers crossed my schedule allows for that. If you love these books, please spread the word. I'm grateful you joined me on this adventure.

All my love,

Kat

ABOUT THE AUTHOR

Kat Ryan is a middle school teacher by day and a budding romance author in the free time she steals for herself. She loves to write about small towns, found families, strong women, and cinnamon roll heroes that love them. She's a sucker for a HEA and more than a bit of steam in the stories she writes.

Kat lives in the Midwest with her husband and her two teenage sons where she consumes a steady diet of coffee, chocolate, and romance books. And while her students and sons plan to never read the books she writes, her husband has and continues to cheer her on.

Want more from Jake and Ivy? Subscribe to Kat's newsletter on her website, https://katryanwrites.com. All "extras" for each of Kat's book are linked in the newsletter that comes out every month.

ALSO BY KAT RYAN

Coming Home

Finding Beauty

Loving Ivy

www.ingramcontent.com/pod-product-compliance
Lightning Source LLC
Chambersburg PA
CBHW021732190726
48288CB00009B/3021